Rude Gal

Sheri Campbell lives and works in London.
Rude Gal is her second erotic novel.

Also by Sheri Campbell in X Press Books

WICKED IN BED

Sheri Campbell

Rude Gal

Published by
The X Press, 6 Hoxton Square, London N1 6NU
Tel: 0171 729 1199   Fax: 0171 729 1771

© Sheri Campbell 1997

Distributed by Turnaround, Unit 3, Olympia Trading Estate, Coburg Road,
London N22 6TZ
Tel: 0181 829 3000   Fax: 0181 881 5088

Printed by Guernsey Press

ISBN   1-874509-32-8

CHAPTER 1

Her long, finely manicured fingers gently massaged his right shoulder as he lay on his side with his back towards her. She felt the tense stiffness of his shoulders as her fingers moved across his soft brown skin, and she began to wonder if her attempts were to be in vain.

Maybe the approach was too subtle, she thought to herself, and decided on a more direct frontal assault. Swiftly her hand moved to the opening in his pyjama pants and sought out the soft warmness of his lifeless penis. Gently gripping it in her fingers, she worked with the determination of a first-aid student attempting to bring life to an unconscious subject. First she played with the member, running her fingers along the shaft and softly stroking its head. For a minute or so she tried this softly-softly method, before moving on to a more active approach.

Gripping his still limp penis in a firm hand she started to work it backwards and forwards in an ever more vigorous fashion. But despite her will to spark life, his dick remained impassive. Her hand movements become more frantic as her frustration at his lack of response steadily grew.

Suddenly she felt his hand grip hers in a gesture for her to stop.

"Look, I'm sorry. I'm just not in the mood at the moment. I've had a bloody hard day at work and I'm really tired." Malcolm Seymour's tone was tinged with anger and his wife quickly withdrew her hand and rolled over to the other side of the bed without saying a word.

In the still darkness of the night, Angela Seymour waited for any further communication from her husband. None was forthcoming. A feeling of anger, frustration, embarrassment and hurt gripped her soul. She thought about asking him if there was a problem, but decided it was futile.

This was hardly a new experience for her, and of late it was becoming an increasingly common one. It seemed that over the last year their sex life had all but disappeared. It had been a gradual decline that had almost begun without her noticing and without any explainable reason. It didn't seem that long ago that they'd been having sex at least three times a week. Now it had got to the point where it was a once-a-month event, and one that for Malcolm was akin to a dental visit. Something that had to be done, but the less time spent doing it the better.

In what seemed like a very brief moment, Angela could hear her husband's slow snoring reverberate into the quiet calm of the night. Cupping the back of her head in her interlocked hands, she lay on her back and stared into the darkness.

Although she was only aged thirty, and had not yet celebrated her seventh wedding anniversary, Angela felt she carried the weariness of a woman fifteen years her senior, and it seemed like she'd been married all her life. She felt old beyond her physical years and, mentally, the coroner could have certified her as dead.

Her mind rewound to the image of a confident, positive, full-of-life twenty-four-year-old, excited about getting married and genuinely believing that the world was her oyster. What had become of that woman? Where had the dreams and aspirations disappeared to?

Angela tried to follow the six-year path in her mind, desperately searching for clues as to what led her off that golden freeway on to the rocky and narrow path she now navigated. In the early years the road had indeed been wide and fast moving. She was very happy with Malcolm, but slowly and without her noticing, her marriage had become dull and confining. Where once it really seemed that no one day was the same; now a week merged into the next, and the months were no more than collections of "thirtyish" days.

Briefly she turned to look at the snoring silhouette of her husband. She again felt angry and shamed at his sexual rebuff. She thought about how Malcolm had the unnerving knack of making her feel as if she was somehow slack and dirty in wanting to have sex with her own husband. On more than one occasion recently he had rebuked her for being "over-sexed" and a "nympho", for daring to make the first move in or out of bed. Each time he rejected her, he was angry, and Angela began to question if the problem lay with her.

Am I doing something wrong in bed? she asked herself. Am I no longer sexually attractive? Had those few pounds she'd put on over the years had a greater effect than she'd realised? She posed the questions but never seemed any closer to finding the answers.

Suddenly she felt very exposed. She wrapped her arms around her naked body. Briefly she lay there with her limbs

3

folded protectively over her breasts. Her nakedness was suddenly a source of her vulnerability. She crossed her legs and turned her back to the man who made her feel so unwanted.

Again her mind focused on the prognosis that her body was overweight and unappealing. Her left hand rubbed her belly to check if it was overly round. Despite her flat, tight stomach she wondered if maybe she should start going to the gym on a more regular basis. The thought that her husband may find her physically a turn-off made Angela feel repulsed, unsettled and exposed.

Gently lifting the duvet, she slipped out slowly and tiptoed across the thick pile bedroom carpet to the door. The sanctuary of the bathroom afforded her the opportunity to stare at her naked reflection in the full-length mahogany-framed mirror on the wall.

She looked at her body and contemplated how her husband saw her. At five foot six inches, she was of average height and so too was her weight. Her proportions were well balanced, with no feature that dominated the landscape. Her breasts were firm and shapely but she wondered if they were "too small".

Angela turned to examine a side profile. She pondered if her stomach was too fat. Her assessment was curtailed by her eyes catching sight of the birthmark on her left thigh. She wondered how noticeable the small, dark, oval-shaped mark would be to others. Her hand ran across the dark brown skin of her right leg, considering how soft her skin would feel to someone else's touch.

At that moment the absurdity of this critical self examination came to her and she sighed deeply out loud and reached for the white cotton bathrobe hanging on the brass hook behind the door.

A small, green-shaded Victorian table lamp bathed the cream-coloured walls of the lounge in a soft and tranquil glow as Angela drew in the smoke from a cigarette. Her eyes surveyed the familiar contents of the room. Beautifully and expensively furnished in top quality period furniture, her three-bedroom St John's Wood flat was the envy of many.

Her family and friends would often comment on her good fortune in finding a man like Malcolm Seymour. As her mother would say, a "good man is not easy to find these days", so she should think herself blessed that she had Malcolm. He was a man who epitomised the old-time Caribbean virtues of hard work and good manners.

In six years he had turned a desire into a reality, and a very successful reality at that. He had started with £2,000, and now had an accountancy practice turning over £1.8 million a year and employing six full-time staff. Mainly specialising in the complex but highly profitable field of mergers and acquisitions, the firm of Seymour, Burgess, Anderson had developed a very lucrative client base and a well respected reputation in the City as a small but very knowledgeable specialist firm.

It was Malcolm's determination to succeed that had attracted Angela to him when their paths crossed eight years ago. They met when, as an administrator at a large Anglo-American bank at Liverpool Street, she had sat next to a new accountant in the canteen. There weren't that many black people working there at the time, and most of those were Americans. She was curious about the 'new kid on the block', especially as he wasn't a Yank, yet seemed so sure of himself.

On first meeting she had thought him rather arrogant, but as she got to know him she realised that his 'arrogance' was just unswerving self-belief and an overriding determination to succeed. After several weeks of lunchtime liaisons they started to go out, and two years later they had married.

To Angela's family, Malcolm was everything they could want in a son-in-law. He was well educated, sophisticated, hard-working, with a good future ahead of him. He looked after their daughter and made sure she had a lifestyle that was the envy of her friends.

Resting her head on the arm of the blue-striped regency-style sofa, Angela pulled another drag from the cigarette before stubbing it out in the glass ashtray resting on the beige Axminster carpet. She was so determined to make her marriage work that she had put up with the continual isolation and boredom of her relationship for the last couple of years. Malcolm was not a bad man, she reasoned, but he loved his work more than his wife, and it seemed as if she would always take second place to his vision of creating a multinational-sized accountancy firm. They seldom had time together these days and when they did, Malcolm was usually too tired to do any more than fall asleep in an armchair. More and more they seemed to be growing apart and Angela felt powerless to halt the slide, while he seemed not to notice it.

When they had married the ten-year age difference between them had not seemed important, but now he acted older than his forty years. Not physically, because he kept himself in very good trim, but mentally he was a lot more conservative than when she had first met him those eight years ago.

Work had become so much his life that the stuffy, uptight culture of City accountancy had started to become ingrained within him. He seemed to spend so much of his waking hours in a grey suit that his personality started to take on the substance of that very suit.

Angela wondered if she was still on life's freeway. Maybe she hadn't really wandered off down some barren byroad, she pondered. Maybe she had just slowed right down and was cruising the slow lane. She had given up on driving her own destiny and had allowed herself to be chauffeured for too long. She had rested in the back seat and watched a driver who had slowed right down when he saw the figure 40 looming up ahead of him. She wondered if she would ever get the car up to full speed again.

The clatter of crockery in the kitchen woke Angela from her slumber. As her eyes focused on the lounge wall she realised that she'd fallen asleep on the sofa. Her bleary eyes tried to make out the relationship of hands to figures on the grandfather clock next to the marble fireplace. Six fifteen, and Malcolm was up and getting ready to set off to his office at Moorgate.

"Hi. You're up early. Are we low on worms?"

Angela tried to put on a happy face and smiled at her husband's attempt at early morning wit. "I thought I'd get up early to try and get some college work done," she lied.

Malcolm sat at the large pine table in their country-style kitchen, scanning the pages of his freshly delivered copy of the Financial Times. A half-eaten bowl of muesli and a cup of coffee lay in front of him.

A large-built man, over six foot tall with neatly cut hair and a pencil-thin moustache, Malcolm Seymour looked every inch the successful black professional man. His mid-brown skin glowed in a way that told the world he was fighting fit and ready to do battle. Immaculately attired in a grey silk suit and crisp white shirt, he cut quite a dash in the City and, being one of the few black faces in that field of accountancy, he was well known.

He loved his work, and today he seemed in even better spirits than usual. Still hurting from her rejection last night, Angela felt an anger swelling up inside her as she looked at his happy morning face.

"Not having it obviously agrees with you," she wanted to say, but could see little logic in starting an early-morning row. If your man doesn't want to screw you, what can you do? she asked herself. Attacking him would not alter the reality. It wouldn't suddenly change how he felt, so what was the point?

He looked so smug sitting there that she just wanted to slap him. Her eyes focused on the bowl of muesli and visualised his reaction of horror and disbelief if she tipped it on to his neatly combed and greased head. Oh, what joy that would be to see, she thought.

"Angie, are you all right?" Malcolm was aware of his wife's eyes cutting into him.

Averting her gaze, she nodded her head and muttered something he didn't catch.

"I'm just tired," she repeated, reaching into the fridge for some orange juice.

Malcolm was on his feet slipping on his jacket while Angela searched for the juice. "Gotta dash. As they say, runnings have to run. See you later, Angie."

She said her goodbye and heard the front door close.

"It's 'haffe', okay? Runnings haffe run." She said it out loud, but there was no one there to hear her.

Malcolm had for Angela the most irritating habit of using Jamaican expressions in the most English of accents. It annoyed her so much because it reminded her of a group of public-school-educated brokers at one City firm where she once worked. In her presence they were forever mimicking a supposed Jamaican accent in the way that only the English middle classes can. It was the type of piss-taking that was not in the slightest bit funny, but she'd had to try and ignore it and get on with her job.

Both Malcolm and herself had parents from Jamaica, but whereas she could slip from her "proper" English accent into patois, Malcolm sounded uncomfortable speaking in anything than his precise, neutral English tones.

Angela poured herself an orange juice and put the dirty crockery into the dishwasher. Lighting a cigarette, she started to browse through a copy of the Voice newspaper. Her eyes focused on an ad on the personal page:

WELL-BUILT BLACK MALE, 28,

FUN-LOVING,

SEEKS SEXY BLACK WOMAN

FOR FUN AND FROLICS.

AGE, SIZE ETC. UNIMPORTANT.

CHAPTER 2

"Yeah, you go ahead and do it and see what you'll get!"

The toddler held on to the video cassette and contemplated whether throwing it was now such a good idea. He paused for a little longer with a defiant look on his angelic face. He examined his mother's face and deduced that his wisest course of action would be to put back the cassette on top of the television.

"He looks like an angel, but he has the heart of a devil. True." June Henry shook her head and watched as her son resumed playing with his red toy telephone. "I'm telling you, Angela, he is a little devil. He must get it from him father. Cos same way the pickney look like saint but act like sinner, so him father stay. True!"

Angela leaned back in the armchair and laughed. As ever, June was on good form, always guaranteed to provide many a laugh. "June, you know I was thinking the other day. . ."

"And you strain somet'ing?"

"Funny! No, I was thinking I've known you for over twenty years."

A look of contemplation crept across June's round honey-coloured face. "Blimey — twenty years! You do less time for murder."

Both women smiled as they took in just how long a time they had been friends. Both their families had lived in Highgate in the sixties and seventies, and June and Angela had met at St Agnes's Roman Catholic School when aged nine. They had become best of friends, and the friendship had remained close ever since.

June was then, and still was, a larger-than-life character. She was always the girl who dared to speak back to teachers if she thought they were taking liberties. It was June then and now who refused to take any foolishness from anyone. In secondary school she would often quote an expression from her mother as way of warning of her intent. "Nah bother come trouble, unless it's trouble yah want," she would tell any person who dared to cross swords with her. Fearless, with a hot temper, June was the sort of person that anyone with any sense gave a wide berth to unless their intentions were good. Angela could remember vividly when, as thirteen-year-olds, a new boy to the school had called June a "coolie" because of her Indian-like features. A hush had gripped the classroom as the children waited for the volcano to erupt.

The poor boy didn't know what hit him. He turned his back for one moment and the next he was lying sprawled across the classroom floor after a large world atlas had made contact with the back of his head.

It was a source of amazement to Angela how her friend had managed to get through school without getting expelled and how she had got through life without having a run-in with the law.

But June these days was somewhat more mellowed. Getting married and having two children had taken some of the fire out of her. But the volcano was far from being extinct.

"So, what made you start thinking about how long we'd known each other, then?"

"Oh, I don't know exactly. I was just thinking how quickly time goes by. The older you get the quicker the years seem to roll by. Before you know it, a year is done. Then another and another." Angela's tone was deep and thoughtful, and it was clear to her friend that all was not a hundred per cent.

June listened, and she became more serious to match the mood. "Ange, is everything all right with you? You haven't seemed your normal self of late."

"Oh, I don't know if things are any worse or any better. More same as they ever was. I can't say I'm very happy at the moment. I'm married to a man who has no time for his wife and who probably wouldn't miss me if he got up and found that I'd gone. I don't think Malcolm has a clue about what I do with my time or what thoughts are in my head. He never asks me about how my college work is going or if I need help. This marketing degree means a lot to me, yet I get no interest, no encouragement from Malcolm. All that matters to him is his work, and he sees my studying as some sort of hobby."

She paused for a moment to sip from her mug of coffee. "I have to be honest and say that my relationship with Malcolm seems empty, but I don't have the strength to do anything about it. I just can't admit it to my family and friends that my marriage is a waste of space. You know how my mother is. She's from that era where if a man don't beat you, then he's a good husband. She thinks I've done the family proud by marrying Malcolm. She's forever telling her friends how her daughter lives in some stush mansion in St John's Wood."

June listened sympathetically to her friend's soul searching. Like Angela, she was married to a man who worked all the hours God gave. She nodded in understanding.

"You know what I'm saying?" Angela asked, seeking approval from her friend.

June looked across at her son, then nodded in agreement. "Tell you the truth, if it wasn't for Layla and this little one, I probably would have left Clive long time ago. Like Malcolm, he's wrapped up in his work and doesn't understand what I need. He's the sort of black man who thinks that it's his job to put food on the table and a roof over him pickney's head. He thinks it's a woman's job to look after the house and pickney. That was the type of home he grew up in, and he really can't see anything wrong with that. At the same time he's a good man and I know that he loves his woman and kids. He's the way he is and that's the way he's always gonna stay."

Angela felt relieved that she could speak to someone who really understood how she was feeling. She'd got up this morning feeling so fed-up with life that she was glad she'd made the trip over to June's house in Crouch End.

It was good to be able to open your heart and chat with a friend who could relate to you and who wouldn't sit in judgement. Someone who would be sympathetic and not tell her that she had nothing to complain about. Angela knew that some of her other friends would think her self-indulgent for complaining about her life; friends who had to deal with the day-to-day struggles of ghetto living thought Angela had it made, and wondered how a woman who lived in luxury and drove a nice car could have anything to moan about. She could relate to that, and she would feel guilty about complaining about an inattentive husband to someone who was raising children on their own and struggling to make ends meet. She knew there were others in situations a great deal more dire than her own, but an awareness of the plight of others didn't make her life any more happy.

She'd once met an old Jewish man on a train journey, who proceeded to tell her about some of the horrific events that had happened in his life. His had been a life filled with some of the greatest tragedies that could befall any individual in a lifetime, yet his message to her was simple: never look for happiness by reminding yourself of the worst things that can happen to the human sprit, but seek happiness by thinking of the very best things that life can give us. Happiness can only be found if we strive to give the spirit the best of experiences.

"Like another coffee?"

June's offer of refreshment stirred Angela from her moment of contemplation. She welcomed the suggestion. While June busied herself in the kitchen, Angela sat on the floor to play with three-year-old Vincent, who was keen to demonstrate his proficiency at stacking a pile of multi-coloured building bricks. Angela made herself comfortable and assisted the young builder by handing him a brick as required. Every so often the little tower would collapse and Vincent would give a small squeal of delight before resuming the attempt.

There was something about June's house that made Angela feel comfortable. A large Victorian terrace in a road of similarly smart, looked-after homes, the house was one of those that the middle-class urban man would retreat to after a day's toil in the office. While Angela's flat was an immaculate showpiece of gracious upper-class living, June's house had a more homely feel to it. It was a family home, and had the familial patina of the wear and tear that children make to a place.

Presently June returned with a tray and handed a mug of freshly ground coffee to her friend. "So, when are you going to join the ranks of the women-with-no-time-for-themselves club?"

Angela looked puzzled, trying to understand June's remark.

Her friend helped her out. "When you gonna breed up the pickney?"

Angela laughed. "June, you've always had such a nice way with words. I can't understand how you never took up writing," she joked. "But it's a good question. I know time is moving on quickly, but I'm not even sure if me and Malcolm will be together in a year's time. A few years ago, when things were good between us, I wanted to have children — but he wanted to wait another couple of years until his business was more established. Now he wants to have them I've told him I want to finish my degree course. Anyway, I told him that the frequency we have sex he would be lucky to produce anything."

June gave a knowing smirk. "Yes, sista. Tell me 'bout dat. I have the same ting from Clive. He's always too tired for anything in the bedroom but sleep. I don't know what it is with these men, yah know. With them bredrin they brag and boast about how they are some sort of bionic stud, but when it comes to the action, they are very slow at rising to the challenge, if you get my drift."

June was having Angela in hysterics. For fear of spilling her coffee she quickly rested it on the pine coffee table.

Delivered in a classic Louise Bennett voice, June's next comment had her friend in stitches: "But, Angela, seriously, it's true what I'm saying. Men have got a lot to learn about what women want. . ."

June hesitated, pausing to think about what she was going to say next. Angela sensed the change in her mood and waited for her friend to continue. "I've never told anyone this before. . . but when Layla was about six months old — well, she's seven in September so it was a while ago — I had an affair. Funnily enough it was that old cliché of the builder come to fit a kitchen. You know Clive's uncle has a building firm? Well, Clive got them in to fit a new kitchen. Remember the kitchen in the old house in Avershan Road? Well, it was that one. There was a guy called Michael who was over from Grenada for three months, and Clive's uncle was sorting him out with work. At first there was another guy doing the work too, but he was unreliable so Michael ended up doing the job on his own.

"Well, Michael was the most interesting and exciting man I've ever met. He had such an enthusiasm for life and an understanding of people. For a twenty-five-year-old he knew more about life than most men will know in a lifetime. I can't explain it, Angela, but I've never experienced a personality like his before and I don't think I ever will again. Every time I spoke to him I felt relaxed and felt that he really understood me.

"The job was supposed to take two weeks. But I deliberately kept changing how I wanted the layout of things, just so I could have Michael around. Clive was

16

going ballistic complaining about how much money I was wasting changing things. But he had no idea what lay behind it. Then, one day, out of the blue, Michael said I should stop changing things around and that if I wanted him there, he would simply do the job more slowly. At first I felt really embarrassed because I hadn't told him how I felt towards him, but I knew he was one man I really could be myself with.

"It was in the middle of summer at the time, and one day it was so hot I was wearing a vest and shorts. At the time I was still breastfeeding Layla, and I was sitting in the lounge giving her an afternoon feed. Michael wanted to know where I wanted a unit located and popped his head round the lounge door. I could see he was a bit embarrassed, but I told him it wasn't a problem if he came in. I pretended I needed to discuss the location of things in more detail.

"I remember that moment like it was yesterday. He was dripping with sweat from trying to move the washing machine and had taken his shirt off. He was wearing long shorts like you'd wear on the beach, and his dark skin just seemed to glisten with sweat. It was the first time I'd really noticed his body. He just seemed so lean and muscular. It really was like some fantasy figure out of a film and all I could think about was what his back would feel like to touch. I was sitting there, breastfeeding my baby, and getting so turned on. . . I was trying to have a sensible conversation but all the time I could just feel myself getting wetter and wetter.

"I could feel my heart really beating fast and my throat was getting really dry. After a little while Layla fell asleep so I took her upstairs to her room. My heart just seemed to be beating so fast and I couldn't work out if I was nervous

17

or excited. I just remember being the wettest I'd been in a long time, so I went to the bathroom and dried myself. I was worried it would show through my shorts. I stopped by the bathroom door and told myself not to do anything I'd regret later.

"When I got downstairs Michael was still in the lounge waiting for me to tell him what needed to be done. He was standing by the lounge window, looking out over the top of the hedge. Some moment of madness must have caught me that day, Angela. I don't know if it was the sun or what, but I went over to Michael and started rubbing my hand over his back. Well, he didn't move or say anything, and for a moment I wondered if I'd made a fool of myself and the man was gonna push me off and tell me to behave myself.

"But, whatever, I just couldn't stop. Next thing I was squeezing his bottom and it felt so good. The guy was seriously cut and he had the sort of body you just want to touch and squeeze. I pulled down his pants and he stepped out of them. He didn't move from where he was standing by the window but people couldn't really see into the room because the hedge was so tall.

"All the while he was standing butt naked by the window and I was squeezing his bum and feeling his legs. It drove me mad. It felt like he was mine to do whatever I wanted to. At one point he started to turn around but I told him just to stay there as he was. I started to rub my pussy against the back of his thigh as he stood there, not moving an inch. I found myself becoming seriously wet and getting more and more turned on by him just standing there. I could feel the skin of his muscular left thigh against my clitoris, and I could sense my wetness on his naked flesh. It was getting me so excited that I could feel my head getting light and dizzy. It really felt like I'd died and gone to heaven. I had my arms wrapped around his waist, gripping him, holding him while I slowly moved myself up and down on his leg. I really wanted to touch his ting but at the same time I was almost frightened to do it. I so wanted to feel him that I thought I'd lose all control if I did.

"I know it sounds strange, because at the end of the day I wanted to have sex with him, but the thought of intimacy excited and frightened me at the same time.

"But as I felt my clitoris getting harder and harder I just had to stroke him. As soon as I held his manhood in my hand I could feel my heart start to beat faster and I just wanted to breathe out loud. It felt so hard that it almost didn't feel like it was flesh. I could feel the tightness of his muscles and the veins so clearly. And I remember at the time thinking that he really wanted me as much as I wanted him.

"Too many times with Clive I've felt that his heart is not really into making love to me. I know sometimes that he does it to please me and not because he passionately wants to sex me. A lot of times he's tired and his mind is still on the problems of his work, so I understand that it's not always easy for him to just get into the sex thing. With Michael I felt that he desired me as much as I wanted him.

As I touched him I could feel the muscles in his penis flex and get harder. I just wanted to hold it tight and feel the blood pumping through its veins. It felt huge, and for a moment I thought about it penetrating me and wondered if it might hurt. I shouldn't say this, but at the time I did compare it with Clive's, and wondered why Clive's penis never felt this hard.

"As I held and stroked his penis I could feel that its head was wet, and it made me think of my own wetness on his thigh. I could hear him start to breathe heavy as I started slowly to rub his ting. He had his eyes closed and his head leaned back, concentrating on me working his penis.

"It felt so exciting to be standing like this in the middle of my front room on a sunny summer's day with a man I'd never touched before. I don't even think that I'd shaken his hand before that day — yet here I was doing these things to him. I felt so wild with an excitement I hadn't felt in years. But the strange thing of it all was that it did feel right at the same time. It felt right that my naked body was touching Michael's and that we were doing this.

"I was starting to masturbate him harder and he was telling me how good it felt. I was trying to keep it going but I wasn't used to using my left hand so I kept wondering if I was doing it okay for him. Meanwhile I was having to slow myself from rubbing on his thigh. I could feel I was getting close to coming and I didn't want to stop working Michael.

"It was such an exciting feeling to feel in control of the situation. I was the one who had power over whether Michael came, and I was in control of when I did too. I could feel that he was letting himself go and was really getting into the whole vibe. He was moaning and breathing really heavily and all the time he was urging me to wank him harder.

"My left nipple was rubbing against his side and it was sending sharp tingles through my body. My nipple was passing milk, and I could see white droplets running down his side to his waist. At times I rested the side of my face near to his shoulder and could feel the sweat of his back on my cheek. He felt so warm, like a person in a fever, and he seemed to be getting hotter and hotter. We were wrapped together with a variety of moistness touching the different parts of our bodies. It made me feel like we were bonded together in a way I'd never felt before.

"Faster and faster I worked his penis, holding his shaft in a tight grip. I could feel a wave washing through my mind as I reached climax. Just as I reached that point I could feel his body shaking and he let out a long, hard moan. At the same time he was climaxing I could feel a powerful orgasm pass through my whole body. I had to hold on to Michael hard, because I could feel my head go light and my legs start to shake. It was the wildest orgasm I've had in my life. At the same time I could feel Michael's body quivering. Both of us just slumped down on to the lounge carpet and lay there holding each other. It felt like a tornado had swept through the house and swept us off our feet. We lay there gasping for breath and he rested my hand on his chest so I could feel how quickly his heart was beating.

"It was about an hour later when I opened my eyes. We were both still lying in the same place on the lounge carpet. Michael was breathing slowly and softly in a mellow sleep. I thought it a shame to have to rouse him, as he looked so happy in his moment of rest. I sat on the sofa and looked at his body. Long, lean, muscular — but as he slept his face could have been that of a child. He had that look of contentment and escape. I wondered where his mind was at the moment, and wondered if it could possibly be any better than where my mind was when I came.

"As I sat there I thought about Clive, but I didn't feel at all guilty. I felt I had just experienced one of the most amazing times of my life. It just felt so right, that I was

21

convinced it was meant to happen. I was amazed that I didn't feel bad, but I didn't. I was so happy and fulfilled. It seemed that for the first time in ages here was someone who really, really lusted after me, desired me.

"You see, having a child destroyed a lot of my confidence. I felt my body was no longer desirable and that I changed from being a woman into being a mother. I don't know for certain, but I sensed that Clive felt that change too. Although he denied it, I think he started to see me differently. I went from being his lover to being the wife and mother of his child. When Layla was born I think something in our marriage died. It's difficult to put my finger on it exactly, but I think I changed and I'm sure Clive altered in his feelings towards me. For a long time I didn't feel at all sexual or sexy. I felt my body was there for Layla and not Clive. He seemed to feel the same way, although he never said anything to confirm it. But I just sensed it. We didn't have sex for about four months, and Clive didn't seem that bothered about it. At first I just thought he was being really understanding, but then I sensed that he wasn't concerned whether we did make love or not. When we did start doing it again, it wasn't as it had been before. The spark of passion had gone. There was no more impulsiveness and spontaneity. Now it seems at times as if Clive is simply going through the motions. His erections aren't as hard as they used to be, and we never spend the same amount of time making love as we used to.

"I have always wondered if Clive has been unfaithful, but he is too organised and thorough a person to ever get caught out. He is the sort of man that would enter into an illicit affair with great pre-planning and have every angle covered before committing himself to any course of action.

Me, I just act on my heart and let my emotions do the talking."

Angela sat, quietly shocked, listening intently to her friend's graphic story. She had never heard June speak so openly and with such emotion before. It was clear that there was a side to her friend that had been hidden to her for many years. She had for such a long time seen June as a mother and a wife, and was surprised to see a more passionate side to this homely persona. It was something of a surprise to hear for the first time that one of her closest friends had been unfaithful. "So, what happened to Michael?" she enquired.JL

June gazed thoughtfully out of the window as tears slowly ran down her cheeks. Within a moment Angela was hugging and consoling her friend. "June, you could have told me at the time, you know. I would have understood," she assured her. "It's strange to hear a side of you that I didn't know existed. You always seemed to have everything so sorted out. I always thought that no man could ever get to you. It always seemed like you called all the shots. I only thought it was fools like myself who let men cause ructions in their lives. I'm glad to see that I'm not the only idiot gal out there!"

June smiled. She understood the humourous sarcasm and felt that a burden had been lifted from her heart. She had held this guilty secret close to her chest for so long that it was a great relief to be able to share it with a friend. It was a long overdue exorcism, and it meant that at last, maybe, she could move on.

For a while the two of them said nothing. Their embrace was a time for reflection and an opportunity for the ghosts of the past to find their own resting place. For Angela it was a moment to contemplate her own feelings of being unloved. It seemed that June had felt exactly the same pain of isolation that she was going through now. It made her reflect that the emptiness of a relationship was something that many of her friends were having to endure. Yet she always thought that everyone else's relationships seemed so contented and together. The grass really did seem greener in those other valleys, yet how things appeared on the surface was obviously no real indication of the real world behind the facade.

She had often envied June, thinking that she was happy with her husband and children. She envied the purpose that having children brought to her life, and had thought it was all that June really wanted. But to hear June talk on such a deep level about a man made her realise that she really did not know what desires and needs were beating deep within her friend's soul.

Angela wondered if she was doomed like so many other women to be stuck in a dry and loveless relationship for eternity. She thought of another friend, Annettte, who for seven years had lived with a man whom she really cared little for. The man was an ignorant oaf, but somehow and for some reason she carried on living with him. She said it was because they had bought the house together and was afraid of being on her own. But in the meanwhile she was having an affair with another guy whom she'd been sleeping with for over five years. She wondered how Annette could continue to live such an existence, content to accept second best for so many years.

June's new offer of refreshment broke the silence. "I think we need something stronger than coffee. I'm gonna have a rum. You fancy something?"

Mindful of the fact she was driving, Angela agreed but asked for a small measure. After fixing the drinks, June looked thoughtfully out of the French windows into the small but immaculately tended rear garden. On the settee her son was softly snoring. She looked at him and smiled. "See, Angela? Typical man. Does a little bit of work and he's tired out!"

"Ain't that the truth," Angela replied, gently stroking the head of the sleeping infant. "Listening to you talk about Michael has made me start thinking about relationships and why we bother having them."

"Well, sista, you have a good point there, yuh know. But it's like the man who goes to the psychiatrist and says, 'Doctor, yuh haffe help me. My brother thinks he's a chicken.' Well, this is a new one to the doctor, so he says to the man, 'How long has he been like this?' The man starts thinking and adding up 'pon him fingers. ' 'Bout ten years, sir,' he says after a while. Well, the doctor looks shocked. 'Ten years, and it's only now that you come to seek my help? Why have you left it so long?' Well, the man looks really humble and apologetic. He is very guilty but has to explain himself to the psychiatrist. 'Well, Doctor, I'm sorry, but we is a poor family and we needed the eggs'! "

Angela laughed and looked with a quizzical eye at her friend. "What the hell are you on about?" she jokingly asked.

"Well, you see, we are like that, man. We know that relationships are madness, but we need the eggs. You know man will mash up yuh head and distress you, but yuh know that yuh need that man all the same."

Angela chuckled and shook her head. She was pleased that June was getting back to her normal form and that her confession of her lost love had been a painful but rejuvenating exercise. "You know, I don't know who's crazier. You, coming out with your backyard theories of life, or me for listening to them," she joked.

"Well, if you can come up with a better theory about why we sistas allow ourselves to get caught up in situations that really don't bring us any happiness in the long run, then you better give it to me."

Angela contemplated the challenge for a moment. "Lord, maybe you're right. Now you mention it, I can't think of too many sane reasons why any woman would get involved with a man," she said with a smile. She sought an answer from her friend. "Do you think it's the same for most women, or are we just unlucky to have men who would rather be at work than in bed with their partners?"

"Nah!" June said, shaking her head. "It's all the same out there. It's just that the sensible ones make sure that there's always the meat and two vegetables at home, but sneak out and buy some chocolate every now and again. Take my advice, Ange. At least once in a while a woman needs to taste somet'ing a lickle bit more exciting than meat and veg. True."

CHAPTER 3

"It can take years to create something yet moments to screw it up, if you pardon my French."

The word "screw" caught Angela's attention, and she stopped doodling on her notebook and looked up at the large display board. Around her, fellow students eagerly scribbled down notes and listened intently as David Salmon, the head of North London University's marketing department, delivered the final five minutes of his lecture on 'Selling the American Dream: The triumphs and failures of marketing in the American automotive industry in the 1970s'.

Now into the second year of a three-year marketing degree course, Angela was finding this Wednesday morning's lecture rather heavy going. She would have been the first to admit that the subject of American muscle cars of the seventies was not something that really awoke her interest in marketing. The hour-long lecture had become a background noise in her head as her mind had wondered back to June's adulterous confessions a few weeks ago.

"It can take years to create something yet moments to screw it up." How prophetic a sentence, she thought to herself as she watched the ginger-haired lecturer collect his notes from the wooden lectern at the front of the classroom.

She was usually a very conscientious student, but today she found it difficult to muster up any enthusiasm. For years she'd thought about taking a break from work to take a degree and was glad she finally plucked up the courage to give it a try.

Since leaving school she'd worked at various City financial institutions and had risen to a well-paid position as a department manager at the giant Allied Pacific Bank in Liverpool Street. The job was interesting and secure, but it was not what she really wanted to be doing and she desperately wanted to move into marketing. But this meant getting the appropriate qualifications and starting her career again.

To her surprise, Malcolm had been very supportive of her decision to go to university, and said that there was no problem financially about her not working, as his business was doing very well.

North London University had an excellent reputation for marketing studies, and Angela was delighted that her application had been successful. She was also pleased to see that she wasn't the only 'mature' student on the course. There had been some trepidation on her part that she'd find herself swapping notes with spotty-faced nineteen-year-olds just out of the sixth form. But her fears had soon disappeared when she realised that there were a fair number of thirtysomethings who'd also wanted to make career changes.

The difference between her and the other students was that, while most of them struggled to make ends meet on the meagre income from part-time jobs and a student grant, she was living well. After the amazed looks she'd received in the first few weeks, she'd deemed it inappropriate to arrive at college in her brand new navy-blue Golf convertible. She'd tried pointing out to one of the more socialist-minded fellow students that it was one of the cheapest convertibles, but it didn't seem to carry any sway. She'd also started dressing down, after a lecturer jokingly pointed out that she could afford more expensive clothes than the staff. Perhaps designer labels were not appropriate for a normal college campus, she'd decided.

After years in the corporate world, suddenly becoming a student had taken quite a bit of adjustment. The fast-moving world of City finance, with its competition, back-stabbing and double-dealing, had been replaced by a world that was a great deal more laid back and a thousand times less stressful. For Angela, going to college was like finding a new lease of life. She enjoyed the friendliness of her fellow students, the challenge of academic studies, and getting out of the nine-to-five rat race. She knew she'd eventually have to return, but at the moment she was free from the strife of City working and enjoying the life of a student. Although she'd have gladly given today's lecture a miss.

As she collected up her things in readiness to leave the classroom, Angela made eye-contact with a fellow student and mouthed a "Hello". Karen Hedges was one of the first students Angela had spoken to on her first day at the campus, and they had since become good friends. An articulate, confident twenty-four-year-old, Karen was the product of a comfortable middle-class background in a small village in Hampshire. She'd worked in Portsmouth for a wine importer before moving to London for her studies. A cheery, happy-go-lucky person, Karen always seemed to be in good spirits and sociable.

She came over to greet her colleague. "Hiya, Angela. How are you?"

Karen's seemingly perpetually smiling face and sunny disposition made her an easy person to like, and on a morning like today's, Angela was glad to see her. She returned the greeting and pointed to her friend's chestnut-coloured hair. "It looks really good — when did you get it done?"

"Oh did it myself at the weekend. I thought it was time I did something with that mousy blonde colour of mine. I thought it was time for the mouse to roar." Karen replied in her distinctive voice. The curious mixture of middle-class home counties and Southampton created an accent unique to her.

On their way downstairs, the two women discussed what they'd each done at the weekend and their thoughts about how the course was going. As they reached the cafeteria, the women joined the long queue of students awaiting a much needed cup of coffee.

The faculty building for marketing and business studies, despite the name of the university, was located in South London's Elephant and Castle area and, having been built in the early eighties, was of fairly modern design and in excellent condition. But the building had been designed to accommodate fewer students than the present admissions, and this at times put a strain on its facilities like the canteen.

Surprisingly for Karen, the queueing was causing her some irritation. "I've never worked out why they don't get a few coffee machines and it would cut down on all this fucking queueing."

"You know that's the first time I've heard you cuss. I wonder what they would say back in Halcyon Acres?" joked Angela. Like the other students she teased Karen, saying she came from the manor in a little stick village.

"You obviously don't know my father. He swears all the time, but I think with his accent no one notices that he's done it. Anyway, I don't think my family are of good stock. I get the impression that my great grandfather made his money selling drugs — opium, I believe."

Angela smiled. "Get out of here! All this time I thought you were a respectable girl, now I discover you're financed by a drugs cartel. Well I've heard of yardies, but this is the first time I've met an 'okay yah-die'!" Angela was at times merciless in her mick-taking of Karen, but she knew that, when Karen was ready, she could give as good as she got.

Karen smiled and was about to give her a witty counter-reply when a young trendy black guy walked past and said "Hi" to the women.

"Oh, Angela. I have to confess, my thoughts were not entirely wholesome when Wayne went by. I know he's but a mere babe — but, my, how quickly children develop these days. . ."

Angela had to concede that Karen was right. "Yes. Wayne has got it going on, but he's far too young for you," she joked.

"Yes, you're probably right," Karen reflected, "but give me a night with him and I'm sure I could speed up the transition from boy to man."

A rather snooty man in front of them turned round and gave them both a look of total disdain. The women smiled at him, and tried to contain their laughter as he turned his back again.

Eventually the women got their coffees and located a table near the large glass windows which overlooked a small paved garden area at the front of the cafeteria.

"You know, Karen, one thing that has always interested me is how come a girl who comes from a village from the middle of nowhere is so down with black guys. I would imagine you with some farmer's boy."

"Yuk! That's the last kind of man I'd want to go out with. I grew up with nerds like that, and they have absolutely no appeal for me. I just prefer men who have a bit of groove and know how to enjoy life. I find more black guys know how to have a good time than white ones. English men are a sad bunch as far as I'm concerned. Too uptight, too repressed, too small-minded, and they take themselves too seriously. I don't even think it's a race thing. I think it's a problem of being an English male. I find other European men totally different. French or Italian men have a totally different perspective to life. But then again it's probably due to the fact that their ancestors were from Africa. Also, I have to say I find black men physically more attractive. My first real boyfriend was when I was seventeen, and he was a black American guy studying at Southampton University. He was such a sexy man that I guess there was no turning back. Once you've tasted honey you really aren't interested in gravy."

Angela was clearly intrigued. She wondered how someone as culturally English as Karen, who grew up in an almost exclusively white environment, should have the perspective that she did.

She had to ask the question. "I hope you won't be offended by this question, but do you find there's a big difference sexually between white and black men?"

Karen smiled. "To tell you the truth I don't know. I've only ever had black boyfriends."

"How did you manage that, living in an English village?" enquired Angela, who was getting more and more curious.

"Hey, just because you grow up in a village doesn't mean you're cut off from the rest of the world. Southampton is only twenty minutes' drive from Fareham. I went out with Laurence, my American boyfriend, for three years before he went back to the States. After that there were three fairly long relationships with guys who lived in Southampton. And that's it: only four sexual partners in my life. Oh, sorry — make that seven. There have been brief flings since I've been in London."

Angela jokingly kissed her teeth. "Well you're no use to me when it comes to doing market research. We sistas are always curious about how the white man measures up to the brothas. I have to confess I've led a sheltered life when it comes to the sins of the flesh. My mummy made sure I stayed a good girl and didn't get up to any 'nastiness', as she used to put it. I've had four sexual partners in my life, including my husband, and all of them were most definitely men of colour. So I couldn't make any comparative studies in regards to the sexual performance of white and black males."

Karen sipped her coffee for a moment then raised her finger. "Ah-ha! Maybe you could suggest the idea to your tutor for your final-year dissertation. You know, a market research plan to discover characteristics of two different market places. I'm sure Brian Lockyer would be delighted to help you out."

"Oh, you've noticed it too? Yes, at first I thought it was just my imagination, but the man is always suggesting me and him should go for a drink to discuss one essay or another. The man is such a wimp: I can't see how he could think I'm going to be in the slightest bit interested."

"Men are very bad at recognising when a woman is clearly not interested," Karen interjected. "Their egos just can't allow them to think that the woman doesn't like them or is not interested in a physical relationship. I find it a problem with male friends. It's difficult because a lot of men just can't put the sexual dimension out of their minds. They are forever trying to get you into bed in one subtle way or another. With some guys I know, it just means I can't relax. I've always got to have my guard up to anticipate a move. There are some male friends that I would never invite for a drink round my flat late at night, because I know I couldn't trust them not to make a move."

Angela nodded her head, knowing exactly what her friend was saying. "That's why I don't have any close male friends. I just can't be bothered to play those cat-and-mouse games. But I suppose the main reason is that when you're married or living with someone it's often difficult to have men friends. My husband would be really funny about it. It's probably because men are such dogs that they know what other men are like. They're suspicious of other men because they know what they'd do in the same situation." She said it very tongue-in-cheek, but both women knew there was a great deal of truth behind the flippant sentiments.

Angela checked her watch and realised she'd have to hurry to get to her two o'clock dental appointment. She finished off her coffee and bid her farewells to Karen. As she rose from her chair a forgotten thought came to Karen's mind.

"Oh, I nearly forgot to tell you. I met a guy the other day who knows your husband. Apparently his firm works a lot with Malcolm's. David Pearce is his name. I thought, what a small world. Oh, and another thing, I'm having a party the Saturday after next, so bring Malcolm along — it would be nice to meet him."

CHAPTER 4

The man was surrounded by heavily armed police, who were slowly approaching his hiding place. Beads of sweat poured from his brow as he surveyed the slowly encroaching officers. He checked the bullets in his pair of revolvers and got ready to make his play. From his cover behind the trees, he shouted to the policemen, "Jus' send out one bad man that can draw," and slowly stepped out from behind the trees and drew his guns in classic wild-west style. A hail of bullets blasted from the police guns, cutting him down.

Malcolm Seymour looked up from his papers at the television. "Angie, could you do me a favour and turn that down a little? I'm finding it difficult to concentrate on this."

His wife took a break from applying her lipstick in the large gilt-frame mirror over the fireplace and picked up the remote control. She checked her hair before depositing the lipstick into the small black leather handbag on the nearby bureau.

Malcolm took a break from his work to peer at his wife. "You're looking very smart. Where did you say you were going again?"

"I'm surprised you noticed. I didn't think I was going to be able to draw your attention away from those papers you're reading. I'm going out with June and Simone to a restaurant in Notting Hill." She examined her make-up and hair in the mirror one last time, and checked that her snazzy black cocktail dress hadn't picked up any fluff since she'd put it on. "Oh, a friend at college knows someone you know. Is it John or Michael Pearce?"

Malcolm looked up and smiled. "You mean David Pearce? Oh, yes." He chuckled. "David and I are old drinking buddies. We've known each other for years."

"And?" enquired Angela.

"What do you mean 'and'?"

"Whenever I hear that rather smug chuckle of yours it usually means that there is a lot more to the story than you're telling."

Malcolm shuffled slightly uncomfortably in his chair, but not enough for his wife to notice. "No, there really isn't any more to the story. I laugh because David is such a crazy guy that if I think about him I think of the crazy stunts he's pulled after having a few. He's one of the best accountants at HBC, who we do a lot of work for. We meet up from time to time and go and have a drink." He paused. "So, who's your friend at college who knows him?"

"Oh, her name's Karen; we're on the same course." Angela could tell from Malcolm's grunt that he'd already lost interest in the answer and was focused back on his papers. "Oh, Malcolm, we've been invited out a week on Saturday, my same friend Karen's having a party."

Angela had to repeat the statement to get her husband's attention.

Malcolm looked at her. "Oh, yes, I was going to tell you that I'll be away in Luxembourg for two weeks to sort out the sale of a pharmaceuticals company to a UK firm. I had hoped to send someone else, but it's too involved to leave it to only one person." He could see from his wife's expression that the news was not welcome.

Angela exhaled loudly. "Okay. Well, it's no big ting. But you could have told me when you got in that you were having to go away. It's always nice to know when your husband is going to be in or out of the house."

She was careful not to lose her temper, but Malcolm could see that Angela was far from happy. He tried to ease the mood. "Listen, I'm really sorry. I was going to say but I really did forget. I'm under a heap of pressure at the moment and sometimes things unfortunately slip my mind," he offered apologetically.

"Malcolm, just every now and again it would be nice if you could remember that you are supposed to be having a relationship with someone — namely me! You never tell me what's happening and you never ask how things are running with me. You don't ask about how my college work is going or even if I'm still at college. For all you know I could have left the course six months ago and become a hooker. You don't know what's going on because you never take any interest. But I really resent it when you can't be bothered to let me know when you're going to be here or not. I just think. . ."

The sound of the doorbell stopped Angela's words in mid-sentence. Malcolm hid himself in his papers as his wife went to answer the door. He recognised June's voice, and was relieved that he'd not have to go through the necessary pleasantries. His wife shouted her goodbyes and headed out the front door.

Outside the immaculate white Georgian house, Angela jumped into the rear passenger seat of June's Saab. In the front passenger seat sat a petite, attractive, ebony-skinned woman.

"Hi, Angie! How ya doing, sis?"

"I'm all right, you know, girlfriend. Simone, where you been hiding yuhself? It's been a long time. . . That's a wicked colour." Angela admired the light turquoise trouser suit her friend was wearing.

"Thank you. I'm trying to start wearing brighter clothes. The old man said I was starting to look like his mum. The man's renk feisty, but I think he might have a point. Oh, and why you ain't seen me in a while is that by the time I reach my home in the evenings I too dyam lazy to move," Simone explained.

A sassy early thirtysomething, Simone could have been mistaken for a woman eight years her junior. Her smooth, slender face was without a line and had the freshness of a teenager's. A legal secretary at a West End firm of solicitors, Simone looked a picture of Essence-magazine sophistication, but her cockney accent said she was very much a down-to-earth sort of woman. She had perfected the art of speaking in the most cultured of tones, then, as she lulled her victim into a false sense of security, she would blast forth in her hard-hitting street tones.

June put the car into gear and drove off along Avalon Park Road, then, turning into Regent's Park Road, she headed in the direction of Notting Hill.

This was the bi-monthly night out of the 'Escape Committee', the name the women had given to their girls-only gathering. They were two members short this evening, on account of journalist Sonia being on holiday and conference organiser Jackie being up in Glasgow on business. But there was enough good vibes to make up for the woman-power shortage. The moment Angela had stepped out of the front door, she'd made up her mind to forget about her annoyance at Malcolm and enjoy her night out with the girls.

They had reserved a table at Red Yellow Green, a trendy new Afrocentric wine bar cum restaurant situated on the old Ladbroke Grove frontline of All Saints Road. Simone had heard good things about the place and suggested the Committee make it their next meeting place.

The cassette in the Saab's stereo system was the soundtrack from the film Waiting to Exhale, and the three women were singing along to a Whitney Houston track in imitation of a scene in the film.

It was an unusually warm May evening, and the three women were in good spirits. Everyone had been looking forward to the evening and taking a break from the pressures of work and family life. It was always nice to meet up with friends, share a few laughs, talk about the old times, and discuss the eternal problems of love and life. Angela felt grateful to have such a group of good friends. They might not have the time to see each other as often as they would have liked, but Angela knew that if she ever needed to call upon their support, they would always be there for her and vice versa. Friends were what made the good times even better and what made the bad ones bearable.

In what seemed like a very short while they had arrived on All Saints Road and were parking up almost outside the wine bar.

"Just think, ten years ago if I'd have said I was going for a drink on All Saints Road my mum would have tried to lock me in the house," observed June.

Simone was in agreement. "Innit!"

The three women stopped for a moment on the pavement to view the new-look road. Where now stood trendy restaurants and designer shops, had been the home a decade or so ago of broken-down shopfronts and illicit shebeens. It was a place where a person would go to score a quarter of sensi, and the Road had an infamous reputation for being a spot where the real rude bwoys could be found. In the present age of crack and automatic guns, those long-past days of ganja dealing by a few dreads seemed harmless and mild compared to the vicious reality of the nineties bad bwoy. Like all things from the past, even the villains seemed better compared to the dread times of the present.

That era seemed so distant now that a wine bar could look trendy if painted in the rasta colours of red, yellow and green. In those days it would have looked like a shebeen or a pattie takeaway.

As they stepped in, the women admired the tasteful and imaginative decor. Bright yellow walls had been combined with old colonial-style furniture and modern fittings to create a relaxing, modern Afrocentric wine bar with the character of the past. The small entrance hid the true extent of the generously sized establishment. To the front were tables for drinkers, while at the back was seating for those who wanted full restaurant service. Despite it being midweek, the place was packed and it was pure good fortune that, as the women arrived, a table at the front was being vacated.

41

Ordering their drinks from a friendly Australian waiter, the women sat back, relaxed, and took in the vibe of the place. There was a surprising diversity to the clientele, with groups of black buppies, white trendies and a few local rude bwoys blended in together.

"It's unusual to see such a mixed bunch of people in the same place, ain't it?" June was forced to observe.

"That's right. London is supposed to be such a cosmopolitan place, but when you check it most people tend to hang out with people who are very similar to themselves. Same race, same class, same age, same lifestyles. It gets boring a lot of the time," Simone agreed.

Angela understood what she was saying, but had her own solution. "That might be true, but it doesn't mean that you have to limit yourself. Your life can be as varied as you want it to be. I think it's that old cliché of life is what you make it."

"Yeah, true. But it's not that simple. For example, look at my family, or even my old man. There are a lot of things that he just won't check because he's already made up his mind that they are not for him. And what he tries to do is make you feel bad for wanting to go there or do that. His set answer is always: 'What you want to go there for? Black people don't go there,' or 'Black people don't do that.' He's so stuck in his ways that it means I don't get to do a lot of things," said Simone.

Angela listened in agreement to what her friend was saying; it was something that she had strong views about. "That's the problem with too many black people — we allow other people to define what we should be about. It's like the sheep mentality. If a few people do the same thing then everybody follows. A few buy BMWs, then every black man thinks that to be a real black man he must drive a BMW. There are not enough people willing to do exactly what they want to do. We spend too much time looking to take the lead from others. But then if you try and do your own thing that is maybe a bit different from the herd, you are attacked for being a coconut."

The sentiments had struck a cord with June, who was dying to have her say. "That is it. That's it exactly. Black people are too damn insecure about their own identity. They too dyam 'fraid to try anyting outside what them already know. Clive's mother, for one. That foolish old woman come to my own house one time and start attacking me for cooking some Russian food. She said I should be cooking rice and peas and that I must not forget my culture. You ever heard anything so foolish? I can cook rice and peas better than that woman, yet she come telling me I should be cooking it for every meal. No imagination," she added. "Clive's not as bad as his mother, but I can see some of the same attitude in him. He likes to take the safe route most of the time and doesn't like to try and sample something that is outside of his experience. We tend to end up going out to the same places all the time, unless I say 'Can we give such and such a try'? "

Angela filled up her glass from the bottle of white wine and gazed across at the table near to them, where a couple of black guys were sitting talking together. The one with a neatly trimmed beard looked across then turned his attention back to his friend.

Simone was really into the topic of conversation, and at such times the volume of her voice rose accordingly. "That's why so many of my girlfriends are single by choice. They are tired of meeting men who can't show them nothing new in life and who have no ambition to try and do things with their life. It's like being stuck on a treadmill, watching the same movie. Women ain't gonna put up with dem ways no more. This the nineties and. . .''

"Bwoy, it must be diss-the-black-man season at the moment, cos that's all I hear the sistas doing at the moment."

Simone had been stopped mid-delivery by the bearded black guy at the table next to them. He had spoken to his friend loudly enough to cut the women's discussion, and with the exact intention of doing so.

Simone was immediately on the defensive. "Excuse me, but me and my friends were having a private discussion here."

The man smiled and raised his hands slightly, offering his palms to the women in a gesture of apology. "Sorry. Excuse me. It was a bit rude of me, but I couldn't help overhearing what you were saying, and as a black man it did cause some offense."

His switch in tone to "charming and articulate" had caught Simone on the hop, and she started to feel embarrassed. "Yeah, well, uhm — no problem." She had made the error of judging him by his jeans, leather jacket and gold jewellery, and made the assumption that she was dealing with a "street nigga", as she would say. Now the man was making her feel uncomfortable.

He leant forward and offered his hand. Simone awkwardly shook it.

"I'm Tony, and my spar here is Frankie." The light-skinned man with the leather baseball cap nodded in greeting. Tony looked at the other two women with a smile. He paused, waiting for Simone to make the introductions.

"Oh. Uhm, these are my friends June and Angela."

Tony shook their hands. "Pleased to make your acquaintance."

Aged in his early forties, Tony, despite his efforts, spoke with a strong Jamaican accent that said he hadn't been brought up in Britain. Angela smiled, intrigued to meet a man who'd been able to spike Simone's cannon. It was not something she had witnessed before. It was clever psychological warfare, and Angela was curious to see more.

He quickly followed up with his counter-attack. "Simone, once again I must apologise for interrupting you. But let me just say somet'ing: it's time black women stopped running down black men all the time. I know that there are problems with some men but, firstly, you shouldn't judge a few and then condemn every one, and secondly, you have to support your brothas, not lick dem down at every opportunity. Everybody wants to knock the black man these days. . ."

Simone was quickly finding her feet and having none of it. "Listen, right, I wasn't knocking all black men. I happen to have a good one at home. But I'm telling you, a lot of you men need to shape up or chip out as far as I'm concerned. A lot of them need to start treating the sistas right and start bringing home some money."

"So, you want a man for his money?" Tony enquired.

"No, I'm not saying that, but there ain't nothing wrong with a man being ambitious and wanting a well-paid job."

Tony rubbed his chin as if pondering the issue like some wise sage. "You know, back in Jamaica there was a rasta called Bongo Dread. Now, Bongo used to have a saying: 'Him who checks for only wealth and not for his spiritual health shall fade away.' People used to laugh at him and say he was just some fool, crazy rasta. Now, one time Bongo was sitting on a chair near a pool room where people was gambling on who would beat who. He used to sit there all day sometimes, playing his drums and reading his bible. But one day Bongo got up from his chair and someone call out, 'Bongo where you ah go?' Well, Bongo said Jah was calling him to go to the nearby gully. Well, a minute later, a lorry came running down the hill and its brakes failed. The lorry, now outta control, drive over the chair where Bongo had been sitting and crashed into the pool room and lick down five people, killing dem stone dead. Now, what does that story say to you?"

"It tells me the MOT standards for commercial vehicles ain't too hot back there, is what it tells me, mate." Simone was growing impatient at hearing this back-a-yard wisdom. "What a load of Bongo bollocks! Man was probably taking himself up to go and have a slash. Call of Jah! More like a call of nature!" she added in her strongest cockney accent.

June tried to muffle her laughter but unsuccessfully.

But Tony wasn't going to give up easily. "Nah, man, you cyan joke about dem tings. There are deeper spiritual things in life that we must search for."

"Yeah, yeah. Tell that to the baby mothers out there trying to raise pickney and pay the bills without no support from the man," Simone hit back.

"Bwoy, I can see that this is one woman I'm just not gonna be able to reason with," Tony declared in defeat. "Now, can I buy you two ladies a drink?" He looked towards June and Angela.

"And mine's a rum and Coke." Simone had regained the higher ground and she knew it. She gave Tony an exaggerated smile and patted him on the shoulder. As she slunk across the wooden floor in the direction of the toilets she paused only to turn and give the man another exaggerated smile.

As Tony took the drink orders, a large grin crept across his face. "Your friend makes me laugh. She's not just extra, she's extra, extra large."

CHAPTER 5

An assortment of multi-coloured lights flashed in time with the beat of the seventies rare groove track. In the middle of the improvised dance floor a group of three retro-dressed soul brothas were shaking down the moves. From the confident way they rode the funk groove they were clearly hard-core clubsters. Occasionally one would dip to his knees and as quickly rise, then execute a perfect spin before letting his shoulders move rhythmically again with the beat of the tune.

Elsewhere in the crowded room others danced the night away in less enthusiastic style, stopping occasionally to consume alcohol from a nearby glass or to roll up a spliff. Despite the welcome breeze from the wide-open windows of the small seventh-floor flat, the heat of so many gyrating bodies pressed closely together made the atmosphere hot and humid. Condensation dripped down the window panes and the white-painted walls.

Angela wiped her brow and regretted wearing a trouser suit to the party. Looking around at the skimpily dressed women, she felt slightly overdressed for the occasion. This rave was definitely a trendy "wear what you dare" kind of occasion. It was not exactly what she had been expecting. When Karen had said she was having a party, Angela had assumed that the majority of guests, like her friend, would be of a more European extraction. But instead it was the brothas and sistas that made up the rank and file at this social gathering.

Angela stood near to the window, where a DJ was setting up his next selection of records, and sipped slowly from a glass of white wine. She tried to concentrate on what a college friend was saying next to her, but the loud thumping speakers nearby made it difficult to hear. Angela's attention to her friend's conversation was made more difficult by the man staring at her from the opposite side of the room. She'd seen him looking at her earlier, but had pretended not to notice. This time she decided to return his stare. It was not out of attraction, more curiosity. Who is this man, and why is he so interested in me? she wondered.

Dressed in worn black leather jeans, scuffed boots and a white T-shirt, he looked out of place next to the smartly dressed, stylish brothas near to him. Around six feet tall, with a well-toned physique, he carried himself with a confidence that came close to arrogance. His dark ebony skin, short cropped hair with long sideburns and a silver earring gave him an attractive air of mystery which intrigued Angela. He leaned against a wall, occasionally putting a bottle of beer to his mouth. His stare was long and hard, and gave no indication of being from a friend or a foe. It made Angela feel both uncomfortable and fascinated at the same time.

Her concentration was broken by a hand touching her right shoulder. "Hiya! You having a good time?"

Angela turned to see Karen's smiling face and returned the greeting. "I love the music, but I have to admit that I remember a lot of the tracks from the first time round."

"Hey, Angela, don't start on that line about how old you feel compared to us youngsters." Angela's six-year seniority in age had been the basis of a running joke between the two women since they'd met on the first day of college. Assuming that Karen was around her own age, Angela had made a joke about the still-wet-behind-the-ears youngsters on the course. She had felt rather embarrassed when Karen told her that she had just turned twenty-four herself. It had been an easy mistake for anyone to make. Karen not only looked several years older, but had a maturity of personality that gave a convincing impersonation of a thirtysomething.

"Well, I have to admit that the thought did cross my mind," she smiled. "It seems that whenever I go out these days the crowd always seems to be just out of school!" She gently elbowed her friend and jokingly enquired, "How come so many of your friends are black? I hope you aren't an anti-white racist."

"You sound like my brother. He's always asking me why I 'hang out with so many darkies', as he puts it. I made a lot of friends through the guys I went out with. Back home most of my friends are from my school days, and they're all white. I guess it's circumstances. Do you think it that strange?" Karen asked with a slight note of concern in her voice.

"Hey, I'm only joking," Angela reassured. "It's just a bit unusual, that's all. I don't have the slightest problem with whoever your friends are, but I do have a problem with that guy over there, whose mummy didn't tell him it's rude to stare." She turned to point out her admirer, but to her surprise he had gone. Before she had time to describe the leather-clad stranger, Karen's company had been requested by a male friend and she disappeared to the improvised dance floor in the centre of the room.

Angela spent most of the party talking to a young photographer called Terry who had some amusing stories of his antics trying to join the paparazzi pack and gain exclusive photos of some Hollywood star or a member of the royalty. His attempts had not been very successful, and he'd decided to try and concentrate on weddings and portraits, as the work was "kinda more regular". He wanted Angela's number, and despite her rebuffs and informing him that she was married, he wouldn't take no for an answer. He was so persistent that she had no option but to give him something that resembled a London telephone number. She felt slightly guilty about giving the number of the Orchid House but figured that, once Terry had got over the embarrassment, he'd probably want to order a Chinese takeaway anyway.

While Terry slipped off to the toilet, Angela decided that it was an opportune moment to bid her leave of absence. She thanked Karen and headed for the front door.

As she went to turn the door handle, a voice called out to her: "Oh, excuse me, sis."

She turned to see a smartly dressed funki dread, his hand outstretched, clutching a neatly folded piece of paper. He saw her accusing look and quickly explained himself. "No, dis ain't my number, sis. There was a brotha here earlier on who asked me to give this to you. The dark brotha with leather pants. . ."

Angela politely took the paper, feeling embarrassed at having given him such a hostile look. She thrust it into her jacket pocket and thanked him before exiting the party.

In the slow descent to ground floor, Angela leant against the lift wall and unfolded the paper.

'Freedom is a road seldom travelled by the multitude. . .'

Let me take you on a journey.

The writing — in what looked like blue fountain-pen ink — was neat and precise. Angela read it again and pondered. A strange thing to write, and without a contact number. What was the point of the note, and why had he not given it to her himself?

As the lift door opened, Angela headed into the warm summer night and tried deciphering the puzzle in her mind.

CHAPTER 6

The house seemed very empty that weekend. Angela had pottered around trying to find things to do with herself, but there was nothing that she really wanted to commit her time to. A college project had been started, but her heart was not in it and she'd given up after scribbling a few notes.

Malcolm had phoned on Sunday morning to inform her that his Luxembourg visit would have to be extended by a further week. She was missing him, yet she knew that, had he been there, she'd probably have seen little of his presence.

Malcolm was umbilically tied to his work. It was his real passion, his reason for living. Angela knew that, if it came to Malcolm having to make a decision between wife and his business, she would be taking the second-place medal. This saddened and frustrated her. There seemed to be no way out of a situation she didn't want. She loved her husband and didn't want to be divorced from him, yet she wondered how long she could continue in this empty no-man's-land of day-to-day existence. There was nothing to do — and this made her frustration grow like a tumour in her head.

She sat on the sofa, staring around the confines of the lounge. She contemplated doing some cleaning, but the house was already in immaculate condition. Their cleaner had come on Friday and had made sure the house was in a state suitable for a royal visit. A copy of Elle magazine provided a temporary respite for Angela's growing sense of boredom. She flicked a few pages, then discarded the journal on to the carpet. Her mood was restless, but she couldn't face the hassle of leaving the house. The television was flicked on and briefly browsed before the remote control returned the screen to its former blank state.

Now, in the kitchen inspecting the fridge's contents, Angela Seymour contemplated the variety of edible options before concluding that her total lack of appetite would prove a hindrance to her enjoyment of any culinary creation she may be tempted to prepare. The fridge door closed, only to be opened a moment later as she reconsidered. Her decision remained as before, but a bottle of ginger ale was liberated and united with some brandy from the bottle next to the blue vase of roses near the ceramic hob.

Lounging back into the soft confines of the sofa, Angela positioned her head on the settee's arm and sprawled out. A remote brought the hi-fi into operation, and a Jade CD started to play. The tall glass of brandy and ginger was a suitable accompaniment to the soft, soothing tones. At last Angela felt herself unwinding and slipping into a state of relaxation.

Her mind drifted off, and in what seemed like a short moment she was restarting the CD from the first track. The alcohol was taking its desired effect, and Angela could feel a mood of deep relaxation start to flow over her. Her mind drifted back to Karen's party and the leather man's rather cryptic message. She had to admit that there was something which intrigued her about this man, but at the same time she told herself that she was not in the least bit interested in him.

Her eyes closed and she drifted into a fantasy scenario which both shocked and thrilled her at the same time. She was back at the same party and was returning the stares of her leather man. Their eyes were locked in a battle of wills, both daring the other to back down and look away. Neither of them did, and Angela was determined to show that she was as much in control as he thought he was. An arrogant bastard whom she would put in his place. She pushed her way through the crowded dance floor in what presented itself as a slow-motion scene from a film. She kept her eyes focused on his as she traversed the dancers, who were all impervious to the duo's battle of wills.

"We're gonna disturb our neighbours, give 'em the full watts tonight," the deejay hollered in the microphone as he turned up the music by many more decibels. The volume of the music dulled and quietened in Angela's head, like a swimmer who ducks into the deepness of a pool and leaves the sounds of reality behind. As she approached him her hand reached out and grabbed his arm. Without saying a word she led him away in the direction of the bathroom, still silent as she bolted the door and directed him to the side of the bath.

Leather man seemed somewhat taken aback by her forthright approach. She had taken the lead, and he had no choice but to follow obediently.

"Kneel down." Her tone was forceful and direct. He did as he was told, and gradually sank down on to the bathroom's carpeted floor. Slowly and deliberately, Angela pulled up her dress and carefully removed her panties. Stepping forward with one hand holding up the front of her dress and the other cradling the back of his head, she brought his mouth towards her mound. Angela felt a shiver run the length of her spine as the warm breath from his mouth blew across the lips of her pussy. Her wetness felt almost uncontrollable, and it seemed like an eternity before the moment she had been desperately waiting for finally came.

The tip of his tongue gently searched for her opening, then found its target. Angela gripped his head tightly, forcing his mouth hard against her increasingly wet pussy. Waves of pleasure washed over her as his tongue thrust deep into her vagina and licked from side to side. Lifting her leg on to the side of the bath provided easier access for his eager, hot probe. Delicately, but with deliberate movements, he worked backwards and forwards into her, his hands gripping her buttocks tightly. Occasionally the sensual rhythm of his movements would be interrupted as he withdrew his tongue and licked the growing firmness of Angela's clitoris.

Her head felt light and her legs started to crumble from beneath her. Supporting her leg high up on the bath tub added to her sense of instability. Her muscles flexed and quivered as she sought to support herself. "Oh yes! Yes!" she moaned as the leather man's tongue thrust deep inside her and found its mark. He was touching her at exactly the right spot, and she gripped his head even more firmly for fear that he may alter the position of his tongue or its pleasurable rhythm. He had got it just right, and there was no way he was going to move from this position unless she wanted him to.

"Suck my clitoris," she ordered him.

Eagerly, with his thumbs, he slowly parted her vagina's lips so as to gain the best access to her swollen clit. He hesitated briefly, as if to make her wait.

The denial was both pain and pleasure for her. Her pussy needed his tongue, but the hesitation brought with it the desperate anticipation that made the eventual arrival all the more exciting.

She could stand it no more. "You bastard! Do as you are told." She would take no further disobedience from her sex slave. She was the mistress, and he had better learn to obey her orders.

She felt his hot breath blow on to the exposed tip of her clitoris, and her spine was close to spasms. He was teasing her, but she decided that on this occasion she would allow his insubordination. From deep inside, a heavy moan found its escape through her mouth as the tip of his hot tongue made brief contact with her engorged clitoris. In slow and deliberate circles his tongue moved gently around her sexual point of being. She wanted him to suck harder but decided that it would be good to be denied for the moment — exactly what she wanted. An image of a drooling wolf came to her mind as she felt the saliva from his mouth run across the rim of her pussy and down between her buttocks.

He was doing very well, she thought to herself. Maybe, if he continued being a good boy, he would get a treat later on.

"Yeah, yeah. That's a good boy. That's nice — you're getting there," she moaned. "That's it. Suck my clitoris a bit harder. . .Oh, that's it. A bit harder. . .Ohhhhh! Yes, yes. . ." Angela could feel herself quickly getting near the point of no return. Before she slipped out of control she pushed his head away from her pussy and moved quickly backwards.

"I need your cock inside me. Hurry up and get undressed," she ordered.

Leather man pulled off his white T-shirt and started to undo the laces of his dark Timberland boots.

"Come on, hurry up," she urged him.

His pace quickened, but not as much as she would have liked. But soon his leather pants lay in a crumpled heap of clothing on the bathroom floor and he stood naked before her. She surveyed him from toe to top, her eyes taking in his well-toned torso and legs before fixing on his growing penis, which quivered as he flexed it, like a light switch — on and off, on and off. . . It was a wickedly sexy cock, she thought, not excessively long but a good size. Its meaty thickness was what she liked, and its symmetrical form was pleasing to the eye. The silky darkness of his skin provided a perfect canvas for the mass of veins that mapped his throbbing erection. The almost total lack of pubic hair showed off his thick knob even better, and she wondered if this was a natural state of affairs or whether he shaved himself.

As her hand gripped his penis she could feel the rush of blood through his veins and the increasing hardness of his member. Gently she ran her fingers along the length of his shaft, taking in the smooth softness of his skin that enveloped a mass of taut muscles. Angela gripped the shaft firmly and watched the skin of his head tighten as the muscles flexed.

She simply had to have this cock inside her, and the sooner the better. Slipping out of her dress, she sat on the corner of the bath and placed her feet firmly on to the floor. Her legs opened in eager anticipation of his wood.

Angela loved the feeling of being in total control, and the more she pushed the limits of her control the more aroused she became. The thought of her bluntness and crudeness turned her on. Her right hand's forefinger slipped into her vagina to bring forth some lubrication to the lips of her pussy. From the hugeness of his erection she concluded that any aid to smooth penetration would be much needed.

When she was ready she barked her orders: "Come here and give me that thing," she said, pointing to his stiffness.

Obediently he moved forwards and, gripping the edge of the bath for support, lowered himself down. Angela wrapped her legs around his waist and, like a spider, pulled her prey towards her. Her legs loosened only so she could spread them wider as the head of his penis came into contact with the entrance of her vagina. Her right hand guided the hardness of his tool into her wetness. Slowly, centimetre by centimetre, she drew his hard cock into her, stopping only to savour the feeling of his manhood flexing inside her. She brought him deeper into her and then braced her hands on the edge of the bath. His manhood was up to its hilt now. She felt the walls of her vagina envelop the firm warmness of his wood. It was pure ecstasy, made only more pleasurable by the slow in-and-out movements he now started to make. Gently he pulled back his penis until Angela feared that it would slip from inside her. Right back he withdrew, until the head of his member was just a small way past her vagina's lips. And just as he drew back, he held his position for a moment, then slowly entered her again.

His movements were slow and deliberate, so she was able to savour the sensation of his penetration taking over more and more of her womanhood. Her eyes were transfixed on his shaft as it made its way in and out of her. It glistened with the moistness of her vagina and made a deviously sexy slurping sound as wood and wetness joined together in a truly erotic union.

His arms were taut, as the limbs' muscles worked to support his weight and he leaned forward in a stoop. Angela's legs gripped his waist and helped lift her bottom slightly from her seat on the bath's corner. The heels of her feet dug into his lower back as she pulled him into her on his forward stroke.

Their movements became more and more frenetic as she urged him to do his required task. "Come on — fuck me. Fuck me," she called out to him, her voice breathy with sexual emotion. Leather man responded with harder, swifter thrusts of his pelvis. Her pussy felt alive with the firm grinding he was administering. Occasionally his penis would enter so deep into her that a strange sensation of both pain and pleasure would send its confused message right through her body. His grunts grew steadily more audible as his body movements became more frantic.

Angela's moaning too had reached higher levels of volume as he carried out her instructions. She rocked herself backwards and forwards in time to his strokes and urged him to greater heights. "Oh, fuck my pussy. Fuck my pussy! Fuck me harder. . . harder! Oh, please, fuck my pussy harder."

He responded by flexing his erection to an even greater hardness, and pumped her vagina with all the energy his body could muster.

But it was still not enough for Angela; she needed him to take her even more. "Oh, yes!" she called. "Ram me with your big cock. Fill me with your cock. Fill my pussy with your dick. Oh, come on. Harder, harder! Fuck me, fuck me! Fill me with your spunk!"

Angela could feel the spasms start from deep inside, as an orgasmic wave of pleasure crashed on to the beaches of her senses. With a deep gasp followed by a moan, she shook as she felt the orgasm unleash its energy within her.
. .

Angela lay on the sofa, gasping gently for breath. The fingers of her right hand rested on the moistness of her vagina. Her black leggings and panties lay discarded on the sitting room's deep-piled carpet. It had been a wonderful fantasy, she thought to herself, and her masturbation had produced a strong and exciting orgasm. She rested her head on one of the sofa's cushions and breathed a sigh of deep relief.

A good, satisfying auto-erotic session was just what she had needed. Now she felt relaxed and contented. For Angela, the pleasures of masturbation had come relatively late in life. She had started at the age of eighteen, and had quickly discovered its wondrous pleasures. She'd soon graduated to doing it in many different positions and locations. She enjoyed many sessions using fingers, a vibrator, carrots, candles and even (on more than one occasion) a cucumber. Whatever took her fancy at the time was brought into play. Malcolm knew nothing about this side of her, and it excited her that it remained an exclusive secret. While her husband was out, she would sit on the floor in front of the full-length mirror in her bedroom and watch while she inserted different items into herself.

Angela was blessed with very sensitive nipples, and would enjoy rubbing them on the cold glass of the bedroom mirror while in a standing position. She especially enjoyed playing with her nipples and clitoris afterwards, when a small amount of cocoa-butter lotion or baby oil would be applied to each area.

Only a few days ago, she had had a delicious orgasm using the shower head in the bathroom. The hot spurting water-blast had sent her clitoris wild with excitement and in a matter of minutes Angela was coming. . .

The loud knock at the front door surprised her and brought her quickly to her feet. She scrambled on the floor for her clothing, stepping into her leggings as she walked out of the sitting room. She straightened herself up and opened the main door. Her eyes met the empty panorama of the salubrious St John's Wood street. She stepped out and scanned up and down the road, but there was no sign of anyone who may have been her visitor. Angela was about to step back inside the house when she spied a gift-wrapped, shoebox-sized parcel, tied with a yellow ribbon.

How sweet of Malcolm to send me a present, she thought as she carefully undid the ribbon. She felt happy that he had at least remembered her while away in Europe, and a smile rapidly broke across her face.

Just as quickly she was stumbling back against the kitchen table, sending two chairs crashing to the floor. A look of absolute horror filled her face and her hand muffled a scream that threatened to break free from her mouth. Her hands shook with fear as she stood and stared with abject terror at the contents of the opened box sitting on the kitchen worktop.

CHAPTER 7

The modern concrete-and-glass building tried desperately hard to be stylish, but somehow could never elevate itself above the level of blandness. Its architect had clearly wanted this building to carry with it some of his creative vision, but financial constraints and local education authority committee collectivism had consigned the University of South London's Faculty of Business to the status of an also-ran in the world of architecture. A few fancy touches of ornate brickwork, several predictably shaped glass windows, and some superfluous multi-coloured exterior pipework could do nothing to conceal the inherent dullness of this box-shaped building.

On the steps outside the building, small groups of students said their goodbyes, discussed some contentious points of a recent lecture, swapped notes, and did what students do. Situated on a busy main road near Vauxhall Bridge, the college building's concourse opened on to a wide pavement which was a main connection point for many local buses. A multitude of bus stops were located outside the faculty, and it was from the almost endless forest of bus-stop posts that Angela Seymour tried to recognise a number that would mean something to her.

Her car was being serviced today, and this was one of those very rare times when she had ventured anywhere on public transport. She had taken the tube to college, but decided to try the bus on her way back home. She wondered whether it had been worth the effort coming to college in the first place. Monday's timetable contained only one lecture in the morning — and today's one had been hardly inspiring. The lecturer had clearly been out the night before, and seemed like he was still recovering. He'd mumbled through a session on problems of audience sampling, and at one point had had to leave the room to get a breath of fresh air.

"Angela!"

Her focus of attention on locating a suitable bus was broken as she heard her name called. She scanned the groups of faces, looking for anyone who may have been trying to attract her attention.

"Angela!"

The voice was louder and obviously nearer, but still she couldn't make out any familiar faces. She was about to walk on to the next bus stop, having decided that the mystery caller was shouting to another similarly named person, when she felt a hand touch her left shoulder.

She turned to see two eyes looking at her out of a black motor cycle crash helmet.

"Yeah, I can see from that look on your face that you're wondering who the raas I am." The man's muffled voice gave her no clues as to his identity. Angela tried to work out who the mystery man was, but she couldn't place him. When he eventually removed his helmet she was shocked to see it was the leather man from the party. She felt embarrassed and surprised.

"Hi, I'm Karl — and I know this excellent cafe not too far from here. . ." He offered his hand by way of a formal greeting.

Angela rather nervously took it and gave a half-hearted handshake. "What are you doing here? How do you know my name? Why did you leave that odd note for me?" Angela tried to play it cool, but the questions just poured forth from her mouth. She could see from the broad grin on his face that Karl was enjoying holding the element of surprise.

"So many questions, so little time!" Even as he spoke he kept that enigmatic smile on his face. "Come — let's have a coffee and see if we can reason out some of those questions," he offered.

Angela could feel the look of indignation breaking across her face, but was stunned by his directness, and for once she was lost for words. Despite her annoyance, she found herself intrigued, and started walking quickly to catch up with him. She was trying to work this guy out, but wasn't sure why she was making the effort. He had the kind of self-assured arrogance that she usually found annoying, and yet there was something about it which caught her attention.

"You really think a lot of yourself don't you?" It was a statement rather than a question, and was delivered with a measure of playfulness that was less than subtle.

Karl turned and grinned at her. He shrugged his shoulders and carried on walking to the gleaming black Kawasaki motor cycle parked up at the kerb. The sporty 1100cc machine had attracted the attention of two youngsters, who looked with awe at the cruise-missile-like machine.

"Wicked bike!" said the smaller, ginger-haired boy. "How fast does it go?"

Karl smiled. It was the question most asked by those interested in motor bikes, and (for someone like Karl, who spent most of his life in crowded city streets) of little importance. "About a hundred and seventy-five. . ."

"Wow! Wicked!"

Karl unstrapped a spare helmet from the machine — but Angela had different ideas.

"You're not serious! You must be mad, thinking I'm getting onto a motor bike. Aren't they dangerous?"

"Yeah, they can be," he said, offering little reassurance. But he could see from the "we are not amused" expression on her face that he would have to adopt a more reassuring approach. "Don't worry. I'm a very safe rider. I've never had an accident."

Curiosity got the better of Angela's inherent caution, and she held him firmly round the waist as the motor cycle pulled on to the busy main road and headed in the direction of Wandsworth.

A mixture of fear and excitement gripped Angela as the powerful motor bike accelerated down the wide two-laned road running alongside the river. Karl was enjoying playing tunes with the bike's gearbox. As he approached a group of slow-moving cars he dropped a gear, blasted the throttle, and overtook at a rate of knots that left Angela gasping for breath. The acceleration of the machine was truly mind-bending, and for someone who had never even sat on a motor bike before, the experience was all the more exciting. The power, and the feeling of being completely exposed, filled Angela with a sense of danger and at the same time a huge thrill. It was not the sort of thing that she'd have agreed to normally, yet here she was being totally daring and reckless. She could just imagine what Malcolm would say if he knew that she'd risked life and limb speeding through the busy streets of London with a man she didn't even know.

Karl slowed the Kawasaki and pulled sharply to the left, outside a small office stationery shop. He told her to wait, and was in and out of the shop in what seemed to Angela like a couple of minutes.

Off they went again, Karl showing off by revving the engine and releasing the clutch quickly. The front wheel rose rapidly off the ground as the bike wheelied for about thirty yards down the busy main road. Angela gripped his waist tightly and cursed him for his crazy antics.

In a moment they were near Clapham Junction and turning down a narrow "pedestrians only" alleyway. Karl kept his finger on the horn and accelerated rapidly down the walkway. Startled shoppers threw themselves against the walls of the passageway as the bike shot past them.

Angela closed her eyes and gripped tightly. Only when she felt the bike coming to a rest and the engine stopping did she dare to open her eyes. "You crazy idiot. Don't ever pull any foolish stunts like that again. If you want to kill yourself, fine — but don't involve me." She was fuming and came close to hitting him.

He put his hands up in a gesture of apology and lowered his head. "Whoa, baby. I'm sorry. Sometimes man mus' tek chance, but I shouldn't have done it with someone on board. Apologies." He helped Angela remove her helmet before getting down on one knee as if to emphasise his apologetic tone.

The passing shoppers who looked on with bemused stares were enough to encourage Angela to make the peace. "All right. Get up and stop taking the piss. Just remember in future that you have precious cargo on board."

Karl rose to his feet with that same grin across his face. "That's beautiful to hear — that we have a future."

It suddenly dawned on her what she'd said, and Angela felt embarrassed. She needed to put him straight at once. "It's a figure of speech. Don't bother getting too excited," she quickly added.

They entered a small cafe through its stripped-pine door, and sat at a small table near the front window. They ordered cappuccinos and Karl smoked a Camel cigarette from the packet in his leather jacket.

"I can't believe that I'm sitting here." Angela paused to sip from her coffee before continuing. "I'm here with some psycho biker who I don't know from Adam. . . I'm married, you know, so please don't get any ideas."

That last statement had nothing to do with the rest, and it sounded clumsy the way she'd blurted it out.

Karl had an enigmatic look on his face. He drew on his cigarette before slowly and deliberately blowing the smoke upwards. "You sound nervous, Angela. I know you're married, and I'm not sure what that has to do with us sitting down here enjoying a coffee together. You should just relax and enjoy the scenery." He had a soothing, quiet and deliberate way of speaking that conveyed a sense of power. Angela had tried to identify his accent, but still could not place it. He was not a street bwoy, but likewise he hadn't been educated at Eton. She couldn't tell if he was from London or outside the capital, or even from the Caribbean. He broke freely into Jamaican patois when the mood took him, so he clearly hadn't grown up in the Outer Hebrides, she surmised.

She looked surprised. "How do you know I'm married?"

"Well, Angela, I always do my research before embarking on any assignment." He said it with a smile, but Angela wondered whether there was any truth in the answer. She wanted to pursue the statement, but didn't want him to know that she was keen for information.

"And what is this 'assignment' that involves me?"

"Sorry, ma'am," he said in a phoney American accent, "that's classified info that's held in the X-files at FBI headquarters in Washington DC."

Angela smiled. "The truth is out there — and I'm sitting here with some idiot bwoy! Answer some questions for me, Agent Leatherman. What is your full name?"

"Karl Malcolm Hendricks."

"As in Jimi Hendrix?"

"No, ma'am — as in Karl Hendricks."

"What is your date of birth?"

"Twenty-fourth of November, nineteen sixty-five, ma'am."

Angela paused for a moment to calculate his age. When satisfied that she'd done her sums correctly, she moved on to the next question. "Why do you think freedom is a road seldom travelled by the multitude?"

"For many, freedom equals fear. Conformity is a safety-net that takes away the need for anyone to think for themselves. There is safety in the herd, but it can be lonely and dangerous for anyone who chooses to wander from the herd."

Angela studied him closely, trying to work out what this guy was all about. He wasn't like the men she normally met. This was someone who was very difficult to place. He couldn't be fitted into the usual pigeon-holes, and that made him fascinating and frustrating at the same time. She was pretty sure his intentions were to try and get her into bed, but as she had no intention of letting that happen, perhaps it would be fine to relax and 'enjoy the ride'.

They sat and talked for another hour about every subject under the sun and more still. She learnt that he'd grown up in Oxford to parents from Jamaica and St Lucia . His mother had died when he was fifteen, and he'd left home a year later when he couldn't get on with the new woman in his father's life. He'd come to London and stayed for two years before buying a motorcycle and heading for Europe. He'd spent the next five years living in various countries before coming back to London. He had done a variety of jobs, including waiting in an expensive West End restaurant.

It had been here that fate changed his life. A group of drunken City types had been at a table arguing about what skills were needed to make it in the Square Mile. Karl, who was clearing their table, had got involved in the discussion and rather foolishly argued that, if he was doing the same trading jobs as themselves, in ten months he would be better at the job than all of them. Sitting at the table had been one of the directors of the Central Manhattan Bank, who had just taken over a large stockbroking firm in the City. As a bit of sport, he'd offered Karl a trial for three months at the firm. Six months later, Karl had been among the top three dealers at the firm, earning more money in an average month than he would in two years of waiting. After years of living from hand to mouth, the cash he'd made in the City gave him a lifestyle he could only previously have dreamt about. He'd bought a Porsche Turbo and a very nice house in Wandsworth. He ate at all the best restaurants, took expensive holidays abroad, and generally lived the good life.

"So why did you pack it all in?" Angela enquired.

"Well, one day when I was coming back from the gym, I saw one of those Nike adverts that say 'Just Do It'. Underneath the text someone had written, 'Why?' That evening I sat down and asked myself the same question. Sure I had lots of money, but I had sold my soul in the bargain. I was spending so many hours at work, and it was such a competitive and stressed environment, that I didn't have time to really appreciate what life was about."

He lit another cigarette before continuing. "In the City, every guy is aiming to be the Big Swinging Dick. That was the name they gave to the top dealer, the guy who walked around the trading floor like he was the don, the guy who was doing the business. Everyone wanted to be in his shoes. Those bastards hated me bad, bad, bad. I was their worst nightmare. A big black guy who they all thought had a bigger swinging dick than them.

"I learnt more about the insecurity of the white male psyche while working in the City than I could have anywhere else. I used to piss them off something rotten. On top of that, there were all those Sloanie women who had never had the chance to speak to a black guy, desperate to find out if the fantasy was fe real. I can remember the guys from work joking about it, but really I could see they were vexed that all these respectable English roses were interested in doing the nasty with a black man. One guy even told me to my face that he wouldn't want to go out with a woman who'd slept with a black man. He probably thought she'd start to make comparisons."

Karl reached into his jacket and removed a black wallet. He handed Angela a small photograph. It was him, sitting at a desk with a phone to his ear. He was dressed in the regulation eighties City uniform: a blue striped shirt and red braces. "I keep it to remind me of the asshole I used to be. It was fun at the time but, as I said, one day I knew I needed to be outta there.

"After I packed in my job I bought a bike, and spent six months going down the west coast of Africa to Mozambique."

Karl's life story was cut short by the waitress, who brought their food to the table. A "quick coffee" had become lunch, but Angela was in no hurry to go anywhere. It was one of those very rare, unexpected kind of days, and she was going to make the most of it. Life had become so predictable that when something came along that broke the chain of normality it was very welcomed.

Angela tucked in to an omelette and mixed salad and wondered if she was doing the right thing by being there in the first place. She found him interesting, but didn't want to lead him on. She yearned for adventure and had fantasised many times about having an affair, but if the possibility ever arose she would always run when it got too close.

"I just realised how you knew I was married and all the other information about me." The realisation had dawned on her as she bit into a slice of tomato. "It's obvious. You know Karen — that's why you were at the party."

"Just like a woman. You've been sitting here all this time trying to make the connection. Well, I have to confess that I didn't have my usual team of private investigators on the case. But, hey, I got the info I needed. By any means!"

Angela smiled, pleased that she had solved one mystery, albeit a rather obvious one. "So, Mr Hendricks, why were you so keen to find out about me?" she asked in a flirty, self-praise-seeking kind of way.

"Well, when I looked across the crowded room at that party, above the booming bass of the music, through the smoke-filled haze of the frenetic atmosphere, I saw a vision of beauty that hit my soul like an arrow. I was mesmerised, and had to cover my eyes. When I opened them, she had gone, so, as I'd already written the note, I thought I might as well give it to you."

Angela gave a look of mock indication and stuck her tongue out. "Oh, you're funny. Or at least you think you are." As quickly as she'd said it the smile vanished from her face and was replaced by a worried and disturbed expression.

"Hey, man, I was only jesting, you know." Karl had clearly seen the change in her mood and offered his hands forwards as way of an apology.

Angela felt an icy chill run up her back, but tried to put on a half-hearted smile. She reached across and held his

73

right hand for a moment. "I'm sorry. It's nothing you've said. It's just. . . something terrible happened to me yesterday." She drew in a long breath as her mind recalled the event. "There was a knock at my front door, but when I went to see who it was there was no one — only a parcel wrapped in gift paper with a ribbon. When I opened it in the kitchen I was nearly sick. It was part of an animal, like a sheep's heart or something. It had an arrow that had been broken stuck into it."

Karl rubbed his chin and shook his head. "Bwoy, that's one rather heavy message. It sounds like someone wanted to say something rather badly to you. By any means."

"Well it scared the life out of me, and I think it was a fucked-up thing to do to someone. The person who did it must be well sick."

It was unusual for Angela to swear, and her doing so now was an indication of how angry she felt.

Karl asked the waitress for the bill and started to put on his leather jacket. "Come, baby, let's shake. I think you need a stiff drink. I know of a place nearby where they do a wicked Cognac."

Angela nodded her approval, but gave him a thorough warning: "Don't even think about playing Eval Kneival. Any more bad-bwoy stunts on that bike and you'll find the passenger seat empty."

CHAPTER 8

The cool-tempo sounds of Miles Davis wafted through the huge loft-apartment-style lounge, and the stripped wooden floors radiated the warm glow of the summer's afternoon sun. The soft, terracotta-coloured, stone-washed walls, huge cactus plants, and large hand-built wooden furniture gave the place a very Mexican feel. The dimensions of the room were truly awesome by London standards: nearly forty feet in length, with lofty ceilings and huge bay windows, the lounge was the main focal point to the house. It was truly stunning, and complemented the rest of Karl's home, all of which had been very carefully and creatively put together.

"Would you like ice in yours?"

Karl's hand replaced the lid of the ice bucket when Angela shook her head. She sat back in the large, comfortable sofa and took in the atmosphere of the room.

"You have a very nice place, Mr Hendricks. I can see a lot of love and time has been spent on it."

"Thanks. But most of the praise should go to the interior designer. I gave her the idea of what I wanted and handed over the money. I have to say we had a few disagreements along the way, but in the end we got there. The house was originally five bedrooms, but I've knocked a couple of rooms together to make the lounge and the main bedroom larger. I'm glad that I saved a lot of the money I made during my City days and put it into this place. I've almost paid off the mortgage on it, so it gives me the freedom not to have to worry too much about making money," he explained.

There was something that intrigued Angela, but when she had tried to get an answer earlier Karl had been evasive. It was time to try again. "You never explained what you actually do now for a living."

Karl shrugged his shoulders. "I never know what to say to people when they ask me that question. I guess you could call me a hustler. I do a bit of this and some of that. I have a few investments, nothing big, and I act as a part-time financial consultant to a few well-heeled friends who, for some mad reason, trust me with their money."

Angela smiled. "That's not exactly what I'd call hustling. I thought you were going to tell me you did a wicked line of Tommy Hilfiger out of the boot of your three-series BMW."

"Nah, man. That's too much like real work for me. I tell you, those guys who do that kind of thing are the real salesmen. Some of those pussies in the City think they are the dons. But get a few of those Brixton hustlers in there and they'd clean up." Karl put his right hand into the shape of a telephone and put it to his ear. "Yes, boss! Jus' give me five million shares in Glaxo, nuh. And if anyone else come fe dem, tell dem yuh nah interested in selling. Yuh understan'? If I hear different yuh have me to deal wid. Seen?"

The bad bwoy accent and appropriate body movements had Angela in hysterics. She rolled about on the settee, trying to stop herself from crying tears of laughter. The two large brandies she'd already consumed helped to make Karl's clowning even more hilarious.

"Now that would be something to see at Morgan Grenfell. I would just love to see how those guys would have reacted if something like that had happened. . . Your glass looks empty, Angela. You need a refuel?"

Angela looked at him with a mischievous smirk. "Karl, are you trying to get me drunk?"

"Who, who, who? Not I, babes. That ain't my style. I like a woman who has all her faculties intact," he said half seriously.

"Yeah, right. I know what men are like. You guys have nothing on your mind but your D-I-C-K."

Karl put his hands to his chest as if her words were wounding him. "No, baby. Don't you be saying those things." He mimicked a black American street accent. "Some of us brothas are new conscious thinking men who have deeper, more noble thoughts towards our nubian sistas. . . Was I convincing?"

Angela shook her head. "Not even remotely. You are a sad case, Mr Hendricks, and I suggest you get the treatment you so richly deserve." She was feeling drunk, and enjoying feeling so. She had the overwhelming urge to be as silly as hell, and didn't care what anyone else thought. She had felt very suspicious and on her guard when she'd first arrived at his house. Expecting a wine bar when he'd said he'd take her to "a place nearby where they do a wicked Cognac", she hadn't known what to think when he'd pulled up his motor bike in the leafy Wandsworth street. But Karl had been right about one thing: the brandy was a cut above the usual. He had opened an expensive vintage bottle, and it really was the perfect finale to the food they'd consumed earlier.

"This 'treatment'. What did you have in mind?"

"Oh, Mr Hendricks! I think you need to be thrashed severely."

"That sounds good to me — where do I sign?" Karl moved from the armchair on the other side of the antique Indian coffee table and sat next to Angela on the sofa.

"Karl, just don't get any ideas. I'm married and don't want any complications."

"I understand exactly what you're saying, and respect your difficult position," he said as his right hand moved and touched her breast.

Angela lay back on the sofa, making no attempt to halt his advances. "You really are out of order, Mr Hendricks. Yah cyan hear what I tell yuh?"

"My hearing isn't so good, but my sense of touch seems to be still functioning."

"And do you like what you feel, Mr Hendricks?"

"Well, Miss Seymour, it does feel fine."

"It's Mrs Seymour, actually. Please don't forget I'm a married woman. And I presume 'fine' means satisfactory, rather than 'most fine'?"

His hand was slowly undoing the buttons of her fawn-coloured silk shirt, and pulling it open to reveal the black lace bra underneath.

"No, take it from me: 'satisfactory' was not something I had in mind when I used the word 'fine'. Believe."

A smile crept across Angela's face as she sunk deeper into the comforting snugness of the soft settee. She could feel his hands reaching behind her back to unhook her bra. She couldn't even feel him unclip the garment, but she felt the warmth of the afternoon sun streaking across her breasts as he lifted the bra off her bosom.

She kept her eyes closed, so she could only guess what he would do next. With no visual distractions, her mind was focused entirely on the physical sensations of his touch. She felt his hands grasp her ankles and spin her round, so that she lay outstretched on her back along the length of the sofa. Her head lay snuggled on a cushion. Well, she thought to herself, if Mr Hendricks wants it, he's going to have to do the work. On this trip I'm going to put my feet up and enjoy the ride.

"Oh, yeah!" The words came out with the breath deep inside her. She could feel the warm wetness of his tongue as its tip circled the nipple of her right breast. As the tingles passed over her she could feel it stiffen in response to his tongue's exploration. He started from the outer edge of her aureola, circling around, then moving nearer and nearer to the centre. As her nipple hardened she could feel his teeth gently bite, then his mouth enveloped her nipple and sucked softly.

Angela's head was awash with sensual feelings which, combined with the alcohol she'd drunk, made her feel like she was floating out deep in space while her body lay grounded on Mother Earth. She didn't want to open her eyes, because in the darkness of her mind she could conjure up all sorts of images and not have to face reality. As far as she was concerned, as long as she kept her eyes closed, what was occurring was happening — but not really happening. Even as he gently lifted her and removed her shirt and bra, she kept her eyes firmly closed.

"Mr Hendricks, you are totally out of order. Totally out of order." She repeated it several times, but it was not said with any degree of seriousness.

Turning his attention to other areas, Karl kissed her neck sensually before working his way to her right earlobe, which he gently bit. Angela lay straight along the length of the sofa, her body relaxing and waiting for its next sensual onslaught. Oh, his hot breath against her neck! It sent shivers through her, the like of which she had not felt in a long time. She never knew what part of her body would be next to experience the stimulation of his hand or mouth, especially now he had removed her ski-pants and underwear. She was now totally naked and exposed to his every whim and desire. Part of her felt vulnerable, but the rest of her revelled in the excitement that this vulnerability brought.

"You like the darkness of the mind?"

She wasn't sure what exactly he meant by that expression. "Oh, it's not dark in here. I can see very clearly. But I'm not seeing through my eyes. . ."

"I know exactly what you mean. Lift up your head for one moment; you might find this easier than keeping your eyes closed all the time."

As she did so, Angela felt the silky smoothness of a scarf being tied around her head like a blindfold. She opened her eyes slowly, for fear that the blindfold might be far from effective, and that the rush of sunlight would spoil the moment. But her concerns were groundless: the material had been adeptly applied to provide a most effective barrier against the bright afternoon sun. Not only that, but the thought of wearing a blindfold filled her with a sense of great titillation. It was not something she had done before, and the sensation was one of total decadence and deviance.

One of the greatest sexual pleasures is the thought of being rude, the feeling of escaping the boundaries of the conventional and the accepted norm. It's like the feeling a child has when she is doing something she knows she shouldn't be, a sensation of wilful naughtiness and an enjoyment of every moment. That was how Angela felt now. She was being totally 'sinful', and loving it. Inhibitions were being dissolved and being replaced by a new realisation that there would be no feelings of 'acceptable behaviour' or constraint — or anything else. She felt slack, and the more slackness the better!

A shriek of half shock and half pleasure jumped from her mouth as she felt a sharp sensation on her left breast. As she focused on the sensation, she realised it was the edge of an ice cube rubbing the tip of her nipple. Drops of ice-cold water ran down the sides of her bosom as the ice melted on the heat of her nipple. The slow circular movements were alternated with the swift lick of his hot tongue. Angela could feel her nipples growing harder to this pleasure-and-pain stimulation. Just as the sensation was getting to its peak in her left nipple, he would run the block of ice down the valley of her breasts and start to manipulate her right nipple.

When the object of the cube's focus could reach no higher pleasure, the ice found itself running across the lips of her vagina. A stream of quickly melting ice-water ran down between her legs and into the crease of her bottom, sending mixed sensations to her brain. The water felt cold, yet she could image it was the wetness from her pussy flowing forth. Before she could consider further, her labia were being gently parted by Karl's smooth fingers and the ice was being rubbed backwards and forwards inside. Like her nipples, her clitoris responded eagerly to the stimulation and firmed to his touch.

As Karl repositioned himself on the sofa, Angela felt the skin of his thigh touch the back of her hand. She hadn't realised until then that Karl had removed his clothes and was now as naked as she was. The urge was now too strong. Angela reached for his leg and used that as a guide for her hand's upward journey. Within a moment her target had been located as she firmly gripped his firmly erect penis. It was strange and wonderfully exciting to be holding the manhood of someone other than her husband. It felt very firm and sizeable, and she had an urge to remove the blindfold, such was her curiosity to see for herself what seemed like a mighty wood. But she decided to remain isolated in her darkened world and use only her sense of touch to help explore this island of sexuality. Slowly she moved his foreskin backwards and forwards along the length of his penis. She savoured every moment of it, feeling his veins rise as he became more and more aroused. She was controlling him through his dick, and she relished the sense of power it gave her. She felt what was going on in his head from the stiffening of his organ. As she stroked the shiny head of his cock she could feel the slippery pre-orgasmic secretions from his dick's hole. Slowly and tantalisingly she stroked the sticky opening with her right forefinger, before raising her hand to her mouth. There, the tip of her tongue teased him by licking the wetness from her finger.

She couldn't believe she was doing this with someone she didn't even really know. She thought for a moment that she must have gone mad — but it was all too pleasurable to care whether she'd lost her mind or not.

Again the urge to remove the barrier to her sight was strong. She wanted to see the look of pleasure in his eyes, but she resisted the temptation. While she remained in darkness, what was happening also remained a fantasy. Reality had never felt this good — so it was better that it remained a slightly alcohol-based fantasy.

She didn't believe it, but the words had come from her mouth. She said it again just to confirm that she'd said it at all. "Karl, I want to taste your dick in my mouth."

Her request was very much his pleasure to perform, and no sooner had the words left her mouth for the second time than she felt the wet stickiness of the head of his penis on her lips. She gripped him with a firm hand and guided the head into her open mouth. His dick felt hot and tasted slightly salty. The tip of her tongue explored the opening as she savoured this new sensation of taste that had been introduced into the game. It felt like a whole new realm of emotions were released as this new sensation became available. Now her mouth sucked gently on his cock, her tongue exploring the curves and lines of its head. She wanted more of his cock inside her so, little by little, she pulled more of his manhood into her mouth. It felt satisfying to have this fat cock inside her mouth. She imagined what it would feel like to have it inside her vagina. Would her pussy be able to take it? she wondered. It felt so very large.

Then she felt Karl pull his wood from her mouth. Disappointment crept over her. I didn't want you to do that, she thought to herself. What was he doing? She felt him climbing on to the settee above her head and wondered what he was planning. And like a baby who'd got its bottle back, she was happy to feel his knob rest against her lips. She opened, and pulled his organ into her mouth. Karl was kneeling either side of her head, adopting the classic '69' position, with him on top.

Yes, yes, yes, she said to herself. The moment that she'd hoped would come had just happened. Her heart was beating faster with the excited prospect of Karl's tongue about to go to work on the moistness of her vagina. She loved having her vagina licked, and she felt like the cat who was about to get its saucer of cream.

But he would first tease her and build the desire within, till she could take no more playing. He softly blew his warm breath up and down the length of her pussy. First he circled, then he went up and down, then he moved from right to left. Angela could feel his breath blowing through her curly pubic hair till he reached the flesh beneath. He came so close that she could feel her hairs touching his lips. When he had teased her enough with his breath he prolonged her agony further by starting to lick her inner thighs. From near her knees to the tops of her legs his wet, hot tongue slowly worked its way up, then down again. Now his tongue came closer and licked around her crotch. He licked the outer limits of her pubic hair but still refused to get to the heart of the matter.

Then his tongue was gone, and she wondered what he would do next. Still nothing happened. Then, suddenly, she felt the tip of his tongue dart across her pussy's lips. Angela sucked his penis contentedly, but her mind had become too fixed on the sensations happening to her mound to focus fully on his cock. "Yes!" she cried out in relief when she finally felt his tongue slip into her moistness. It was probing deeper and deeper inside her, and she could feel the firmness of his hands as they held her inner thighs. His grip slowly parted her legs to give him greater access to the nectar in this honey pot. His tongue sought the furthest reaches of her vagina and he explored all the innermost recesses of her now very wet orifice.

Shivers of tingling pleasure shot through her body as he went to work on her sex. Somehow, without having to tell him what to do, he was carrying out cunnilingus exactly the way she liked it; just the right amount of pressure was being applied by his tongue, and he stayed at each spot just long enough to arouse to the maximum without over-stimulation.

She adored the way his tongue massaged the length of her clitoris, stroking it and filling her head with the most wonderful sensations she could imagine. He started gently to suck her clitoris while alternating a rubbing action with his tongue.

Karl was slowly undulating his hips so the head of his penis slipped backwards and forwards in her mouth as if he was inside her pussy. Occasionally her left hand fondled his hanging sack. His hip movements were becoming stronger, and she had to grip his dick more tightly so that it would not go too deep into her mouth. It was as stiff as a board and seemed twice as long.

"Oh, suck my pussy, suck my pussy," she said to herself, as ecstasy rose within her soul. She wanted to shout the words aloud but those throbbing inches of hard cock she had in her mouth made any form of verbal communication out of the question.

"Yeah, that's the spot. Come on, just suck it like that. Oh yes, you big dick, lick my pussy out. Lick my pussy. That's it, that's it, just a bit more. . . . Taste my pussy juices. Eat me."

She talked in her mind only, imagining that she was saying the words to this wonderful pussy-sucking man.

Normally it took a fair amount of stimulation for Angela to climax, but suddenly she realised that she was about to come. It had arrived slightly unexpectedly but, like the surprise of a good friend turning up at one's door, it was most welcome. An almighty rush came to her head as she felt the powerful orgasm grip her. Her pelvis convulsed as the pulsating waves of ecstasy flowed through her. She felt her heart beating rapidly and had to withdraw his penis from her mouth as she gulped for oxygen and let a moan of pleasure escape from within.

Her right hand pumped his cock, urging it to relieve its burden. Her wanking was fast and frenetic, and in what seemed like a mere moment she felt the tool flex in her grip and a jet of hot spunk squirted over her lips and down her cheeks. As Karl let out a deep groan, Angela worked the torrent of sperm from his cock with long, hard strokes. She felt the need to have his cock inside her mouth again, and a finger inside her vagina, so she eagerly pulled his manhood into her and sucked the last drops of semen from him. As she did so, her finger rapidly did its much-needed duty and swiftly brought on another wave of orgasmic pleasure.

The clatter of a coffee cup was the first sound she heard as she awoke from her sleep. The blindfold still on her face and the feel of the sofa's fabric on her bare skin made her realise that it was not a dream. She removed the scarf. As her eyes became accustomed to the new intensity of light, she took in the form of Karl walking over to the hi-fi. She noticed the coffee cup on the table near the sofa.

Karl read her mind. "The shower is running. I thought you would like to freshen up."

The hot torrent of water was exactly what she needed. The shower-head blasted new life into her body as she tried to shake of the myopic effect of the alcohol. The afternoon's proceedings replayed in her mind several times as she tried to recall every moment. Yes, it did really happen, she thought. That really was me.

She tried to feel guilty for being unfaithful to Malcolm, but somehow the self recriminations just weren't forthcoming. She felt guilty about not feeling guilty. She had to accept that she was feeling damn good about the afternoon. There was a radiant glow inside, like the sort one gets after hearty exercise or pulling off some minor achievement.

"Fuck it. I feel good," she told herself out loud. It felt for that moment like someone was letting her have a second burst of her carefree, youthful days. She felt twenty-one again, she felt desired, and she felt like a woman. A horny, attractive one at that. The words of James Brown's I Feel Good were playing in her head and she couldn't resist a little wiggle of the hips as she soaped herself.

Fully dressed again, and sitting with a mug of coffee on the sofa, it almost felt like she'd run a marathon in record time. She wanted to poke her head out of the lounge window and yell to the passers-by below: "Hello, people. I just had a fantastic orgasm and I wanted to share the experience with you. Bye!"

Though Angela wanted her excitement to get the better of her, Karl seemed somewhat distant. He spent an unnecessary amount of time selecting a compact disc to play. He would examine the cover notes of each possible selection with the care of someone who looked as if he had never read them before.

"Karl, you okay?"

He turned and smiled and she felt a lot happier.

"Yeah, I'm fine. That was quite a session." Then he paused and walked over to the leather jacket lying on the floor near the armchair. "I bought this when we stopped earlier at the stationer's."

He handed her a brown paper bag which contained a large diary. "What I want you to do is, for the next seven days while you husband is away in Luxembourg, I want you to record the times we have together. I want you to note down every detail of our passion, so that it is indelibly inscribed in your mind for the rest of your life. You see, Angela, I know that when your husband returns this will all end and you will go back to being the dutiful wife. . ."

"Hold on a minute, Mr Hendricks. Aren't we being a bit presumptuous here? Who says this wasn't a one-off? I might regret everything badly."

"Do you?"

"No. But who's to say I might not have? You really do rate yourself, don't you?" It wasn't a serious question, and it was said partly in jest.

"Well, all I know is that we had a damn good time, and I don't think you are ready to not come back for seconds."

"Karl, I have to admit that you did offer a reasonable level of customer satisfaction. But how do I know that you'll be able to repeat the performance, and that I won't get tied into buying some product that I don't need in the long term?"

"Madam," he enthused in a pseudo-American salesman's accent, "I can rightly understand your concern at being lumbered with a product you don't rightly need but for a limited duration. But rest assured, at the Hendricks Corporation we understand the needs, desires and concerns of our customers. As a result, we offer a fixed period in which you can use then return our product. Also, we offer a special money-back guarantee if you are not completely satisfied."

Angela smiled and shook her head. "Seriously, Karl, I'm not going to do this when my husband returns. You understand?"

"Hey, I ain't got any problems with that. Don't worry, you won't get any grief from me. It ain't my style."

"How did you know my husband was away in Luxembourg?" Angela enquired, changing the subject.

"I think you mentioned it earlier."

Angela rubbed her head. "See how pissed I am? I can't even remember what conversations we've had and we only met today." She looked at her watch, and was surprised to see it was 7.00 p.m. "Shit! Listen, I better be going. Please can you call me a cab?"

"Angela, you're a cab."

"Bwoy, you tink dis is time for jesting!"

Minutes later the cab driver was sounding his horn outside.

"Angela, you have my number. Am I going to see you again?"

As she walked to the door she blew him a kiss. "I'll think about it."

CHAPTER 9

"I don't believe what I'm hearing. You're winding me up."

The incredulous look on June's face said a great deal more than her words. She lowered the glass from her mouth without even taking a sip. When she got confirmation, her hands clapped together excitedly.

"Go, girlfriend, go!"

She could still not quite believe what her best friend was telling her. She'd always thought of Angela as a bit of a 'goody two-shoes', and was now having to re-evaluate her views. The two had met at Cafe Lea in Covent Garden before a planned day's shopping. It was a bi-monthly ritual that they would meet up West before murdering their credit cards.

Angela confided most things with June, and her liaison of the day before was not going to be an exception. She'd told June all about Karl, and how they had ended up making mad and crazy love in his lounge.

"To be honest, Ange, I always thought I was the rude gal in this dynamic duo, but dis time yuh gone clear. I didn't think you would get involved in an extra-marital affair at all. But I must say, it sound plenty exciting." June let out one of her trademark belly laughs and clapped her hands to emphasise her point. "But Ange, you aren't starting to have regrets or any foolishness like that, are you? Cos, girlfriend, you know my thoughts on that matter long time. Every woman deserves a little bit of adventure at least once in her life. True?"

"No, I'm not having no regrets or anything like that. I don't really think that Malcolm cares enough about me to owe him any heavy-duty pledge of fidelity. To be honest, I wouldn't be surprised if Malcolm's had a few affairs in the time we've been married. And I think you're right: I do deserve a bit of escapism. But for some strange reason I don't want to end it with Malcolm, and I would be shattered if this broke my marriage up."

"Ange, why you saying those tings? Why should this mash up your marriage? You ain't gonna do anything foolish like go and tell Malcolm, are you?"

"You mad, June! Of course I'm not going to say anything about this. You think I like trouble, girl?" Angela paused for a moment to gather her thoughts. "It's just, you never know what goes through the mind of some men. They are quite happy just having a ting with a woman and defining the relationship as 'casual', but when the woman tries to do the same thing they don't like it."

"Yeah, too right. Their egos can't take the idea that a woman might just be wanting them for sex. But as you say they are quite happy to have a woman for their own pleasures. What's good for the goose ain't good for the gander."

Angela looked to catch the waiter's eye and ordered another coffee and orange juice. Cafe Lea was, as usual, the bustling cosmopolitan place it always was. Popular with Covent Garden's arty designer set and tourists alike, the cafe started to get close to bursting point around this midmorning time of day. The women were glad that they'd got there before the rush began.

Angela plunged a fork into her carrot cake and levelled with June about her fears. "It is a risk I'm taking, because I don't know anything about this guy. You've seen Fatal Attraction, haven't you? That's all I need — the reverse happening to me."

"Cho, sounds more like fetal attraction to me! If this guy is like the typical black man, then he'll think he's hit the jackpot and nah even haffe run!"

"The 'typical black man'. Does such a thing exist? And if it does, somehow I don't think Mr Hendricks would call himself that."

"White man, black man, coolie man, thief. Dem is all the same. Dawg! Is just dat some are better housetrained than others."

Angela had to laugh. June was, as ever, her usual irrepressible self. She said the most outrageous things and somehow managed to get away with it. Politically correct or liberally minded were not concepts that one would associate with this larger-than-life woman. But somehow it was delivered with such humour that Angela would always forgive some of her very un-nineties comments.

"Check that there." June pointed at the trendy, suited, tall, black thirtysomething reading a copy of GQ magazine at a nearby table. "He thinks he's really some of that. He's that type of guy who will think that they are the nineties new man and are a cut and a half above the yard man in the street. But don't be fooled by any of that fancy packaging. When you get down to it, all men are the same. Trust me."

"June, that's the most outrageous generalisation I've heard you come out with. You don't even know anything about that poor guy, and yet you are making these terrible accusations."

"Some are better housetrained than others, that's all."

Angela didn't really think her friend was being serious, more arguing a point for the sake of contention than out of conviction.

"Ange, I have to admit I'm not being totally serious. As you say, some is good and some is bad. Anyway, you told me that this guy worked at Goldberg Sachs. . . Well, my friend Marie has been there for ten years and works in the trading department, so she must know him. I'll quiz her later and see what the four-one-one is on Mr Hendricks."

"Yes, let me know what she says. He's done his homework on me, so it would be good to be able to get something on him."

June looked serious for a moment, and Angela could see she was about to offer some stern advice.

"All I say to you, Angie, is be careful. Just remember that the stakes are high in this game, and if you mess up you could regret it for the rest of your life. Jus' remember, girlfriend, that this is a bit of fun and that's it. Just make sure you tell the guy straight that after this week then it's all over."

"No, June. You're totally right and I know I've got to be careful, but I don't think Karl is going to give me any trouble. He seems like a pretty together kind of guy."

CHAPTER 10

Dear Diary,

I met Karl last night and we rode on his bike down to Richmond and sat by the river and had a drink. He was in a good mood, talking about a trip he wanted to make on the motor bike to Hungary later on in the summer. We had an amusing time talking about our fantasy black government and who should be in which cabinet post. Later we went and had pasta at a nearby Italian restaurant and I decided that I would give up the rest of my week to indulging myself on one long sexual adventure. We named it The Week of Living Dangerously, and even made a toast to it with a bottle of champagne.

I told Karl that he shouldn't drink and drive but, as ever the rebel without a cause, he dismissed the law as a mere technicality. He certainly likes to 'tek chance', as my mother would say, and obviously enjoys being slightly reckless. I suppose that this is why I was sexually attracted to him in the first place. It's the unpredictability that I find so appealing. You never can guess what will happen next.

June is right. I am taking a massive risk messing about with this guy. It could cost me my marriage and a very secure (BUT BORING!) and comfortable lifestyle. But after years of always doing the sensible thing, I think it's time that I thought about myself and my needs.

I just can't keep going through the same old routine day in day out. I feel at times that I could die of boredom in my marriage and I'm not sure how I can rectify the situation. So the arrival of the leather man is my chance to have my own adventure. I have decided that I'm going to use this week to explore my own sexual fantasies and try all those things that I never quite got round to.

I suspect that Karl has a slightly kinky side to his sexual personality and I find that exciting. I doubt if he would call it kinky, he'd probably see it as just being adventurous. He really does believe that the expression 'Freedom is a road seldom travelled by the multitude' applies to all areas of the human experience.

Last night really was the perfect summer's evening. The ride on the way back to his house was great. It felt like I was on holiday, cruising along the river and through the green lanes of Richmond.

I could seriously get into this motor bike thing. It just feels so wild and exciting. I just love that feeling of power and acceleration and not having to wait in boring queues of traffic. (I wonder if I could persuade Malcolm to get one. JOKE!)

When we got back to his place we sat out in the garden and took in the warmth of the night. The garden has been created by a landscape designer and it really feels like you're sitting in the countryside. We took a bottle of chilled wine outside and sat on the two lounger chairs he has out there. It felt like I'd left London and was sitting in the garden of a cottage in the countryside.

I sat there taking in the warm atmosphere of the night and the perfumed aroma of the various flowers and plants around us. Once again I could feel myself getting a bit tipsy and feeling rather giggly. We started to play a game of general knowledge, where he would ask me a question, then I'd ask him another. If either of us got one wrong we'd remove an item of clothing.

Why is it that when you've had a few drinks the answers to what should be simple questions always seem so hard?

Needless to say, getting the capital of Colombia wrong got me down to my panties and bra. Having said that, I'm not sure that Karl wasn't deliberately answering incorrectly so he could get his things off. I messed up the next question and had to take off my bra.

The night air was very invigorating and made my nipples become very erect. This fact wasn't missed on Karl, who was now taking off his last piece of clothing. (What is the largest African state? His answer: Peckham.)

He stood by the side of me and started to rub the head of his dick on my boobs. He was obviously feeling very horny because his head was shiny with juice. He squeezed some out on to my nipple and massaged it in with his dick.

He wanted to take off my knickers but I told him he hadn't asked me a question. "As the square on the hypotenuse is equal to the sum of the squares on the other two sides, which of them stays at home, does the washing and looks after the kids?" I told him, "Both," but he claimed it wasn't the mathematically correct answer and that I'd have to take my panties off.

It's amazing what a warm summer evening can do for a woman. When he put his finger into my pussy I was surprised at how wet I'd already become. Probably a combination of the wine and being outside that made it more difficult for me to judge how wet I was.

There is something so exciting about being outdoors naked at night. It felt totally natural, yet naughty at the same time. It's a secluded garden, but I'm sure that the neighbours could have seen us if they'd happened to have looked out of their windows. But that added to the whole thrill of it all.

What is it with Karl and cold things? (Not that I'm complaining.) He poured some of the wine from the bottle over my nipples and it ran over my belly and down between my legs. He seemed to get very turned on by it. He was licking and sucking my nipples with such excitement that it rubbed off on me. I thought I was going to come right then.

He'd got wildly excited by this point and I asked him to put two fingers inside me. He has very long and smooth fingers, nicely shaped and (for a man) immaculately manicured.

I have to say his fingers really turn me on just looking at them. Inside my pussy they are even more sexy. I gripped the arms of the chair and raised my bum up a little bit to get a better view of his fingers fucking my pussy. I could feel his fingers getting deep inside me and my wetness helped make such a horny slurping sound.

Occasionally he would stop with his fingers inside and use his thumb to stimulate my clitoris. It was driving me wild. I told him I wanted more and he kindly opened me wider to insert another finger. I was laying back and really opening my legs wide to accommodate his digits.

I was moaning so much that I'm sure half the neighbourhood was probably looking out of their bedroom windows by then. The night's full moon would have greatly aided the illumination of their own personal peep show. To tell you the truth, I was having so much fun by then that I really couldn't have cared in the slightest who was peeping.

That crazy finger-fucking was getting too much, and I had to take a break. Karl squeezed up close to me on the lounger and started to kiss my neck and nibble my ears. When I felt his tongue inside my mouth it made me feel that I was floating above the two of us looking down. I know the expression "I thought I'd died and gone to heaven" is a rather overused one, but I couldn't think of anything more apt than that to describe how I felt at that moment. I have no idea how long we lay outside exploring each other's bodies, but I lost track of time altogether.

When Karl slipped off the chair and rolled on to the lawn laughing, I took my opportunity. As he lay on his back making some observation about the brightness of the moon, I quickly straddled him and started to stroke his cock. I gripped him in my hand and slowly started to masturbate his thing. I found it very satisfying to feel his hardness grow to the point where his cock felt like solid muscle.

My intentions were totally selfish, I have to confess. All I wanted was to get that hard flesh inside my cunt. (I always used to think 'cunt' was a crude word, but Karl has helped me discover how wickedly sexy it really is. Thank you, Mr Hendricks.)

I moistened the head of his penis with my saliva, then carefully lowered myself on to his manhood. I had to let out a gasp as that massive cock of his filled me up. Even after having those three fingers inside me, it still felt like a stretch to take him in. But oh, was it a good feeling or what! There's another cliché about size not mattering, but, hell, it does make a good fuck of a difference. Karl's cock is so thick and hard that I could feel his veins touching the sides of my pussy.

I started slowly sliding myself along the whole length of his tool from top to bottom. I would lift up till his tip was just past my cunt lips, then I'd gradually lower myself down savouring each moment, every inch of his member. His hands were on my breasts, teasing my nipples and sending sparks of pleasure down my body. I started to move quicker as the urge to fuck this man to death gripped me stronger and stronger.

I was fucking him with frenzied passion that felt out of control. I rode his cock with ever swifter and harder strokes, and *his dick was getting so deep inside me. I was coming down so hard on his penis that I wondered afterwards how his balls took the pounding. I felt powerful and in charge and enjoyed being the jockey on this thoroughbred stallion, urging him past the post.*

"You like this pussy? You like this fucking I'm giving you?"

I was shocked to hear myself say the words, but say (or shout) them I did. Not only that, but I started to curse him and enjoyed doing it.

"You bastard, you fucking dirty bastard! I want your spunk inside me. I want your hot spunk inside me," I grunted at him through gritted teeth. I was already at this stage vigorously rubbing my throbbing clitoris with two fingers. I can't recall ever feeling it so swollen and hard before, and I knew that I couldn't keep the tidal gates back much longer.

My cursing sent Karl over the edge, and almost at exactly the same moment that the first waves of orgasmic pleasure swept over me, I could feel Karl's hot seed shooting inside me. I felt his pelvis convulsing as he let it all go.

I rolled over on the grass, exhausted, our bodies covered in sweat and tingling with pleasure. We lay there for quite a while, staring up at the stars, neither of us saying a word. At that moment I really realised what a good fuck was all about. I think that's when it. . .

"I'm surprised you're still enthusiastic enough about marketing to come here after that last lecture. . ."

Angela hadn't seen Karen approaching and, hearing her voice, it had startled her. She swiftly pushed the sheets of paper back into the diary Karl had given her, and tried to adopt a normal composure. Sitting in the quiet confines of the college library, she had immersed herself in writing up the journal, as Karl had requested. She'd decided that the allocated space in the book, although generous by normal standards, was not enough to do her wild sex session justice, so had started to write on sheets of notepaper.

She suddenly realised that the speed in which she'd reacted just now must have looked very suspicious. "Oh, hi! Enthusiastic or what?" She wasn't sure quite what her friend had meant.

"I saw you really engrossed in writing up your notes, and I started to feel guilty for sleeping through most of the period."

Angela had to agree that the morning's lecture had been far from inspiring. A long-winded and tediously technical monologue about the market for electrical white goods in the UK, it had been an ordeal. Barry Cox was never an entertaining lecturer at the best of times, but today he'd made the talking clock seem engrossing and witty.

"You were lucky you could sleep. I'm sorry, but that Barry is a seriously dry man. I can't believe that someone so dull has kept his job."

Karen nodded in exaggerated agreement and warmed up to start on her favourite subject, lecturer bashing. "Yes, but what about some of the others. . ."

Angela could see where the conversation was heading, and she had been down this road enough times to know the terrain off by heart.

Karen certainly had a bee in her bonnet about the college lecturing staff, and how she loved to take any opportunity to slag them off. Angela guessed that there was something about her that disliked authority, and being critical was her way of getting back.

Angela showed her disinterest by concentrating hard on an opened text book, and Karen got the hint. A lull in the conversation followed, as Angela continued to feign interest in the book and Karen thought about how she should best approach her next topic.

"How are things going with Karl?"

It was not a question that Angela had been expecting, and for a moment she was uncertain how she should react. She didn't know what Karl might have said to Karen, and was embarrassed that her friend may know she was having an affair.

Karen had sensed the unease that her first question had caused, and sought to ease the situation by asking another one. "I hope you didn't mind me telling him your name and what you did?"

"No, it wasn't a problem. Karl is an interesting person and I'm sure that we could be good friends." Angela was treading a safe middle ground, wondering what her friend knew while at the same time not saying anything too incriminating. While she considered Karen a friend she was a relatively recent one, so it made Angela uncomfortable to be talking about Karl. The last thing that she wanted was to become the centre of gossip around the college about her conducting an affair. As she had discovered many times in the past, the world was a small place — or, more accurately, the black community was a very tiny island.

She all too well remembered the situation of June's cousin Roger who, as a musician, was often out on the road touring with various big-name pop groups. Roger had started to cheat on his woman and thought that, as the liaison was happening in Leeds and his woman lived in London, there was no chance of his infidelity ever being discovered. Unfortunately for Roger, his lover's best friend happened to be related to his wife. Well, gossip had soon spread and in a matter of weeks his wife had packed her bags and flown from the matrimonial lovenest.

Time and time again Angela was discovering that every one of her friends knew someone that had some connection, however tenuous, to herself.

So she hoped that Karen would drop the subject, but her friend obviously wanted to carry on fishing.

"So, are you just friends. . . or something else?"

Angela smiled and decided that it was best to avoid telling the truth. "Hey, we're just friends. Nothing more. Why are you so interested, Karen? Are you and Karl having a thing together?"

"Oh, I had a brief thing with him a long time ago," Karen confessed, "but we are just pals now and I don't want anything more than that." She paused as a memory came slowly back to her. Her left hand supported her chin and she stared off into the distance. "Karl is the type of person who turns his friends into lovers. Slowly but surely he winds you in like a fish, and bit by bit you end up in the net. The man has a lot of charm and knows how to use it for his own ends. You see, Karl is like the self-made man who worships his own creator. He loves no one more than himself, and likes everyone to love him the same. He gets into people's heads and can really mess you up."

As Karen stopped and reflected on what she was saying, Angela lifted her gaze away from the book. "It sounds like you had a bit of a heavy time with him."

Karen shook her head. "No, not me. I made sure I kept myself out of any deep involvement. No, it's just things that other women have told me about Karl. I knew someone who went out with him for about a year, and she got really in love with him. He let her get into that situation even though he could see what it would do to her. And, of course, when she got fucked up, he simply looked for his next challenge and told her that it was her own fault as he'd never made any promises. Well, this woman had got so involved that she came close to having a nervous breakdown. And of course Karl never saw that he had done anything wrong. He just thought that if some silly bitch wants to mess up her head, then it was her problem."

While Angela was interested to hear what her friend was saying, at the same time she really didn't want to get involved. She was enjoying her moment of escapism with Karl and was happy just to enjoy the ride. She saw it as a brief encounter, and had no intentions of anything serious. She wondered for a moment whether Karen was telling her own story.

"Hey, don't bother giving me any warnings. I'm just friends with Karl and I'm quite happy for things to stay that way," she stated. "I'm married and have every intention of staying that way." Angela squirmed. The thought of adopting the hypocritical persona of a saint filled her with an acute sense of embarrassment. She didn't like lying, but couldn't afford to let gossip start.

Karen gave a smile that left Angela unclear as to what she was thinking. All the same Karen seemed happy with her friend's answer, and it was clear that her involvement with Karl was more than the passing fling she had told Angela about. "Oh, Angela, let me tell you what happened to me yesterday. I was in the King's Road when this really distraught old woman came up to me in tears and said she had lost her purse. I was asking her where she thought she had left it in an attempt to try and help her find it. Then she starts to say to me, 'Give me back my purse.' Well, the woman was obviously a bit dotty so I started to walk off. Now she started to follow me, shouting and begging for me to hand over her purse. I went into a shop but she followed and I got so embarrassed I had to leave.

"I was walking as quickly as possible to get rid of this woman but she kept following me, crying and pleading with me. Everyone was looking at me as if I'd robbed this woman but, typically for London, no one bothered getting involved. For once I was glad about that.

"I managed to jump on a bus and escape, but I was really stressed out for the whole day. I kept wondering why she had picked on me. It really spoilt the day for me."

"That's terrible." Angela sympathised with her experience and thought about her sister Janet. A couple of years before, her younger sister had been wrongly accused of stealing a shirt from a store on Oxford Street. The store detective had manhandled her back into the shop and proceeded to humiliate her in front of the other shoppers by making her empty her bag on to the counter. There was no shirt in the bag and the detective realised he had made a mistake. Normally Janet would have created hell with the store manager, but she was so shaken and embarrassed by the incident that all she wanted to do was to get out of the place as quickly as possible.

"You're not the only one to have had a strange experience recently. . ." Angela proceeded to tell of her disturbing delivery of an animal's heart with an arrow through it. Even now as she relayed the story she could feel a cold shiver run down her spine and a sick feeling in the pit of her stomach. Exactly the same sensation she'd felt that day. The box's contents had been a horrible shock to the system, and being clueless as to the perpetrator's identity left her feeling very uneasy.

A look of disgust registered on Karen's face as she listened to her friend's unpleasant delivery. "What a sick, horrible thing to do. Some. . ." Karen's words were cut short as her attention was caught by the occupant of the nearby study table. She'd noticed a fellow student staring across at them, but he had looked away when her eyes made contact. "Now, there's someone who you could list as a likely suspect," she said, her head nodding in the direction of the table in question.

"Patrick? Nah, he doesn't strike me as the sort at all. Now, if my panties had been stolen off the washing line, maybe!" Angela joked, not convinced that Patrick Knowles was the culprit.

A quiet and introverted man in his late thirties, Knowles was the kind of social misfit who would have seemed more at home on the platform of a regional railway station than on a marketing degree course. Fellow students had nicknamed him 'the Trainspotter' because of his misfit ways and liking for staid and unfashionable clothing.

"He's a member of the archery society, you know," Karen said, further developing her case.

Angela looked harder at Knowles, deliberating if this new piece of information changed her previous perception. She pondered for a moment longer before giving her verdict: "Circumstantial evidence. What about a motive?"

"Maybe he has a fixation on you," Karen suggested. "You must notice the way he's always staring at you."

"Well, I'm not convinced. He stares at every woman, and I don't think that I'm number one in his fantasy woman league. Anyway, he's harmless. I've spoken to him and he's just very shy and introspective. I'm just surprised that he's doing a course like this one. He says he doesn't want a job in marketing, which is just as well cos I couldn't see anyone employing him."

"Harmless?" Karen was having none of it. "That's probably what they said about the Boston Strangler. His school report probably said: 'Lovely boy, good with his hands. . .' "

Karen and Angela spent another hour and a half in the library, discussing love, life, the pursuit of happiness, and occasionally something to do with the course work.

Later that afternoon Angela drove to Battersea to pick up some material she'd ordered for new curtains in one of the spare bedrooms. She liked to keep the flat in tip-top condition, and always made time to keep things looking good around the home.

On her way home to St John's Wood she stopped off at Bryant's, an agency which specialised in domestic cleaning. Angela's regular cleaning woman was moving to South London, so she needed to sort out a replacement. As the saying goes, it was hard finding good domestics these days. After a couple of terrible cleaners, the Seymours were glad to have found Stella, but now they would have to start all over again. Angela parked up outside the small, former tobacconist's shop on the busy Kentish Town Road, then headed to the reception desk.

"I have an appointment for a cleaner."

The middle-aged receptionist stopped typing on the computer keyboard and glanced up. "We're not recruiting any staff at the moment, dear, but if you leave your name and contact details we'll keep them on file."

Angela took in a deep breath and tried to maintain her composure. "No, I'm not here for a job. I have an appointment to arrange for a regular cleaner for my house," she stated calmly but coldly.

The woman's face turned a deep shade of crimson as she wiggled uncomfortably on the typist chair. "Oh, I'm sorry, dear. It's just that we don't get. . ." She stopped mid-sentence, as she realised the likely repercussions of what she had been about to say. "Err, take a seat. I'll see if Miss Edwards is free. . ."

Angela was still pissed off from her reception at Bryant's when she arrived at her mother's house in Enfield.

What a rahtid cheek! she'd thought to herself all the way there. She sat in the car for a few moments to compose herself before knocking on the front door. Her mother had not been too well of late, and she wanted to be in a good mood to greet her.

"Hello, darling! I didn't think that you'd reach so soon."

Angela hugged her mother and handed her the flowers she'd bought on the way there. "Hi, Ma. How you feeling?"

Mrs Rhone put a hand to her chest and sighed. "I have to give thanks to the Lord that I'm a lot better, but the doctor tells me that I have to watch my blood pressure."

In the bright afternoon sun, Angela Seymour was suddenly struck by how much older her mother seemed. Even though it had only been a fortnight since she had last seen her, today she really noticed the effects of time and her recent illness. She had lost some weight, and her hair seemed to have greyed a touch more. Her weight-loss had in turn added more lines to her face.

When you watch your parents growing old you start to realise how quickly life can pass you by. You blink, and five years have gone. You close your eyes for a moment and a decade has waved you bye-bye. While many would say that at thirty years old Angela was at the prime of her life, she could remember her twenty-first birthday like it was yesterday.

What was starting to worry her was that time was moving so quickly it seemed that it was going to rush by and leave her behind. To many of her friends she had 'arrived', and didn't have to worry at all. But to Angela, all this meant was that she had married a man who was successful. But what had she achieved in her own right? Not only that, but what had she experienced of life? There were so many things she'd not done, so many places left to visit. If the world was a stage, then it seemed at times as though she was still waiting for an audition. Life was about living, experiencing, growing; there were no guarantees about how long you had to sample it, and so it made sense to try whenever possible to live each day as if it was your last.

That was a philosophy that Angela was beginning to realise related more to her view of life than her husband's. Malcolm was obsessed about the long term, and seemed to forget that the future was only made possible by the present. Being the wealthiest couple in the graveyard was of little interest to Angela, especially if it meant you had to sell your life to pay for it.

"Where's Dad?" she enquired as her mother switched on the kettle in the kitchen.

"Oh, him gwan to see his friend Norman in Brixton."

The many years in Britain had tempered Marceline Rhone's Jamaican accent slightly, but, as she often said, she was born a Jamaican and would go to her grave as one.

Her husband Cecil had recently retired and was taking the opportunity to meet up with old friends he'd not seen in a while. The couple had been married for thirty-eight years, and had strived to provide a good home and education for their four children. Like so many of their generation they had seen good and bad times. They had left Jamaica full of expectations, only to face the cold reality of Britain in the fifties. The newly-weds had been forced to live apart for nearly a year as they struggled to save up enough money so that they could rent a house together. Through hardship and adversity they had raised a family any parents would have been proud of, but the struggle came at a price — namely Mrs Rhone's health. Angela was inspired by what her parents had achieved against the odds, and in comparison to the hurdles the black community faced today she realised that her generation had it relatively easy.

Angela took her cup of coffee and retired to the comforting confines of an armchair in the lounge. She kicked off her shoes and stretched out at ease in the familiar surroundings.

A large, Edwardian terraced house in a quiet tree-lined street in Enfield, the Rhone home represented many years of hard toil. Immaculately decorated and furnished, it was exactly the home that Marceline Rhone had always wanted. To others it may have seemed a modest goal, but for Marceline and many others of that generation it represented in part what the struggle to make a life in Britain was all about. That, and the fact that all of her children were doing well in their chosen careers, filled Mrs Rhone with much pride.

She joined Angela in the lounge and proceeded to give her daughter the latest gossip on what was happening to all the family and friends. And if there was anything that Mrs Rhone liked above all else, it was a good gossip.

"Well, my dear. You know my friend from the church, Hyacinth? She'll be coming round in a moment. Well, her eldest boy, Winston, has gone an' get 'imself in trouble with police. Stolen cars or somet'ing like dat. Him has caused a lot of grief and shame for his muddah. . .

"An' your uncle Alton in Florida is getting married again to a woman thirty years his junior. Him mus' want a short-cut to him grave. . .

"But I don't know how they can allow the pastor back home after 'im turn homosexual. . .

"I don't wan' call nobody a liar, but I don't think truth has seen that woman's doorstep fe a long time. . .

"All I can say is, when dat woman fell out de ugly tree she haffe hit every branch. . . "

The subject-range of gossip, as usual, spanned the encyclopedia of human experience and crossed the vast expanse of the black diaspora. Third cousins twice removed living in Guyana to friends of distant friends who had emigrated to Chicago. . . all came under scrutiny from Mrs Rhone.

Angela sat back and laughed at some of the ridiculous stories, pausing only to question her mother about the authenticity of some of the more incredible tales. The only thing that she hadn't heard from her mother's never-ending collection of gossip was any family member who had been abducted by transsexual aliens. She made this observation to her mother, who kindly reminded her of cousin Neville in the Bronx. He had been found naked and drugged-up in a New Jersey motel without his wallet, watch or clothing. He'd claimed not to know how he'd got there, but could vaguely remember a bright white light and strange figures in shiny silver suits. Well, whoever these 'aliens' were, they'd quickly grasped the workings of the humanoid monetary system. Later that day his 'abducted' Amex card had been used to buy women's clothing to the value of $1200 from Bloomingdale's department store. . .

Angela nodded. Okay, she'd forgotten about that one. And she had to accept that the 'alien' could have been a transsexual. In fact, knowing of Cousin Neville's sexual peccadilloes, she'd bet evens that it was.

A knock on the front door ended the session of family misfortunes.

Mrs Rhone led her guest into the lounge.

"Hello, Mrs Bailey," Angela greeted the formidable-looking woman. An extremely large woman in her late fifties, Hyacinth Bailey helped to redefine the term 'mampy', and elevate it to even greater heights. Her navy dress was of such proportions that it could have doubled as stage curtains for a large theatre. But her size defied all current medical theories, as she was always the very picture of good health.

She warmly greeted Mrs Rhone's daughter and accepted her offer of refreshment. As she settled on to the sofa, her vast proportions gave the three-seater settee the appearance of an oversized armchair. She had been to the house many times before, but she would always make the same comment as if it was the first time she was saying it: "I mus' say, Marceline, you have a lovely house. And always so very neat and tidy."

Even though she'd heard it many times before, Mrs Rhone couldn't stop a small smile of pride breaking forth. "T'ank you, Hyacinth. Like all things I'm grateful for what the Lord has provided."

"Amen," Mrs Bailey responded. "He has truly provided very nicely for you."

Mrs Rhone could detect a touch of envy in her friend's remark, and this made her even more pleased. The two women were long-standing friends from the Holy Spirit Triumphant Evangelical Church based in Edmonton, North London, and were among the leading lights in the church. Wherever there was a committee needed to organise some event or fundraiser, the two women were always there.

"Oh, Ma. I just remembered the unwanted clothes you asked me to bring. . ." Angela popped out to her car to remove a large black bin bag, and dragged it through the lounge door.

Mrs Bailey's fat fingers delved into the bag and pulled out a black and gold sequinned cocktail dress. She dived in again and removed two other similar items of clothing. It was too much for her. She burst into a loud belly laugh, which always had the effect of causing a similar response from Mrs Rhone.

Angela gave both women a puzzled look. "They may be a little eighties now, but they're not that bad, are they?"

The remark sent Mrs Bailey into an even greater bout of mirth and in turn Mrs Rhone followed suit. Presently Mrs Bailey was able to compose herself enough to bring her chuckling under control. She rested her hands on her heaving bosom and tried to take in some breath. "Oh, excuse me, dhaling. I wasn't laughing at your clothes. Well, I was. . . but more for what dem needed for."

When Mrs Rhone had asked her daughter for any unwanted clothes she may have had in her wardrobe, it had slipped her mind to explain exactly what church project they were needed for. Angela had assumed it was a jumble sale, but now, as Mrs Bailey explained the Clothes For Africa Appeal, she could understand the reason for her mirth. A French Connection mini cocktail dress was probably not the most sensible of clothing items to send to small rural villages in the Sudan.

"Cho! I thought I'd got rid of those things for good," moaned Angela.

The Mercedes shot out of the side road without the driver looking properly. Angela slammed on her car's brakes just in time to avoid smashing into its side. The male driver dropped the mobile phone he had pressed against his ear as he realised what he'd done. Angela was about to tell him about his mother when he offered up his hands in a gesture of apology and she took pity on the fool. His ashen face gave the impression of a man about to have a heart attack. Embarrassed, he sped away into the early evening traffic.

What is happening to the drivers in London? she thought to herself. There seemed to be a growing number of people who thought that the highway code was to be used in an advisory capacity only. This was becoming one of those days that she would rather had not happened.

As she drove down the Finchley Road, her thoughts ran back to comments her mother had made after Mrs Bailey had left. Marceline had routinely asked how Malcolm was, and then proceeded to tell her daughter how fortunate she was having a husband like him. Her mother's words had made Angela feel slightly guilty about what she was doing with Karl. She wished she could tell her mother about how she felt in her marriage, but she knew there was no way her mother would understand. She was from a generation which believed that marriage was for life, and that a woman's lot was to grin and bear it. Concepts such as feeling self-fulfiled would be alien to her mother, who would see them as self-indulgent and airy-fairy. Mrs Rhone could deal only with tangible things. To her, Malcolm was a good husband because he provided very well for her materially. He didn't hit or abuse her, and he showed respect. For a generation who had had to struggle just to provide a roof over their heads and food in their bellies, one was grateful for what material luxuries hard work and good fortune provided. Marriage, Marceline would say, was about creating a family and building security for old age. It was an institution that involved responsibility and commitment to others, and was not about individual satisfaction. It was like national service — something you did for the greater good of other parties. Self-sacrifice was a concept that everyone adhered to and understood. What she didn't realise was that later generations had begun to take certain material standards as a right, not a luxury. For these subsequent generations there was more to marriage than just getting your own home and having children. They wanted and demanded more.

Angela reflected on how much things had changed in such a relatively short time. Changes so rapid that it left her, like so many of her contemporaries, unable to discuss many issues with her parents. She reflected on her mother's life and her own. Her mother, who had slept with only one man in her life — and that was after they had married. The idea at first seemed difficult to comprehend, but when she thought about it longer, she realised how little she'd known about sex before she'd married Malcolm — and how little she still knew.

She parked the car in a space a few doors down from her house, removed the radio facade, took the curtain material from the boot and walked to the front door.

Two bills, a bank statement, a postcard from a friend on holiday in Morocco, and leaflets advertising an estate agent and a pizza delivery firm, awaited her arrival on the hallway mat.

She went straight upstairs to run a bath. Back in the kitchen she poured an orange juice from the fridge. A quick look through the mail, and she pinned Sonia's postcard on the small noticeboard above the washing machine. Then she added some Malibu to the orange juice and opened the fridge again to see what was there for an instant snack. She took out some pitta bread and houmous, checking the 'use by' date on the packet. It was yesterday's date, but that was not a problem. She put two small pittas in the toaster.

It was good to be home, thought Angela. It always was. It was a safe haven from the crazy day-to-day madness happening out there in the big bad city. The pitta bread was too hot, so she left it to cool for a moment, glancing at the items on the credit-card statement. Who was G&H Ltd, London W10? Oh yeah, the picture frames. She dipped some bread into the houmous, then walked to the front room to play her answerphone messages:

"Hello, Angie. Just a call to see what you're doing. It's June, by the way — in case you forgot the voice. Laters."

Beep.

"This is Valerie Edwards from Bryant's. I think I have a cleaner for you. The only problem is her English is a bit rusty. But she's from Africa, which I thought you may prefer. I'll phone tomorrow."

Beep.

"Hello, darling. Sorry to miss you. I hope everything is going well. I'm sorry, but I'm going to have to spend another four days in Luxembourg sorting this deal out. It's a lot more involved than any of us realised and we've being working some ridiculous hours trying to get it together. Hope you're not too bored without me."

Beep.

"Your time is nearly up. . ."

Angela rushed over to the machine and played the message again. The caller had used some sort of voice distorter, which made their voice sound like that of a robot. She played it a couple more times. It was impossible to tell the age, sex, or anything in particular about the voice. In frustration and anger she played it time and time again. Then, in fury, she knocked the answering machine on to the floor.

The questions went backwards and forwards in her head. Was this someone playing a joke? If it wasn't a joke, was it the same person who'd sent the package? But who the hell was it?

CHAPTER 11

A beautiful, warm, sunny summer's afternoon. The breeze blowing into the slightly opened visor of Angela's helmet was heaven. Karl was cruising the big Kawasaki at a steady 50 mph, and the world was a wonderful place.

The long, straight highway, bordered with woodland on either side, was the perfect road to be travelling along at that moment. As a roundabout approached, Karl blasted past a slow-moving car then took a sharp left into a road that ran straight into the forest. The roads became narrower until Karl was gliding the motor bike down a tiny dirt path deep into the woodland. When they eventually reached a shady glade Karl brought the superbike to a halt and rested it on its stand.

Angela removed her helmet and took in the beauty of the summer's day. It had been a long time since she was last at Epping Forest. Only a short ride from the noisy and polluted streets of East London, Epping could have been a million miles away. Only the faint, distant rumble of traffic was a reminder that the city was never that far away. Rays of sunlight were diffused through the overhanging branches of the forest trees, and the small clumps of greenery were washed in bright sunshine like an oasis in a desert.

If London represented lifestyle, then this was life, Angela reflected. It was the perfect way to spend a sunny afternoon, and she was so glad she'd taken up Karl's offer.

From the panniers of the Kawasaki, Karl was busily removing a large, checked tablecloth and several plastic bags. In a short while he had laid out a rather impressive looking picnic, complete with a chilled half-bottle of champagne and two cut crystal flute glasses.

"Madam, luncheon is served." With a white napkin draped over the arm of his black leather jacket, Karl played the maitre d' and showed Angela to her 'seat' next to an old cut-down tree stump.

The jerk chicken with potato salad, coleslaw, plantains and coconut rice went down a treat with a glass of chilled bubbly.

"To love and life," Angela proposed, raising her glass in way of a toast.

"Peace, power and pussy," suggested Karl instead.

"I'm not going to make a toast like that," said Angela, withdrawing her glass.

"Okay, okay." His mood was conciliatory. "Pussy power!" He raised his glass to a sneer from Angela.

A loud kissing of teeth was her reply to his cheek.

"It's what makes the world go round," Karl theorised. "No, seriously, it's what drives men to achieve and be successful. And women know that shit and they know how best to use the most effective assets nature has given them."

Angela was tutting, clearly not impressed with Karl's line of reasoning. "What is it with you guys? Why are you so basic? Isn't there more to life than just tending to the needs of your dick?"

"Uhm. . . uhrm, I don't think so!"

Angela smiled, not taking him seriously at all. She sipped the chilled champagne from her glass and lounged back to take in the pleasant warmth of that tranquil summer's afternoon. There was a peace there that was the perfect antidote for the stress and strains of urban living. It was a time for relaxing and just chilling out. Nice and easy. Overhead a dozen swallows darted and glided in the blue, cloudless sky. Angela gazed upward, her eyes trying to follow the birds' swift, erratic movements.

Karl, meanwhile, was piling a paper plate with various items of food before he summoned her attention and passed it over. As she tasted the well-presented fare, it crossed her mind that Karl had gone to a lot of trouble to prepare the picnic.

"Who was that comedian on the tape you were playing?"

Angela had arrived at Karl's earlier in the day, and had spent a few hours chatting and enjoying the sunshine in his back garden. Karl had been busy getting the food ready and fixing a couple of things on his bike.

"Oh, the one I quickly turned off when you arrived?" he said with a grin.

"Yes. I did wonder why you did that."

"Tell you the truth, I didn't think you'd find the Dice Man too politically correct. To say the man is slack is an understatement. He comes up with lines like, 'I was seeing some bitch recently and she says to me, "Give me twelve inches and hurt me." So I fucked her twice and hit her in the head with a brick.' Or, 'I was seeing this bitch that was such a tramp that I had to double-park my dick on her ass and wait an hour before I could get in'."

Angela kissed her teeth in disapproval. "Well, it's just as well you switched the tape off. It sounds like more woman-hating slackness to me."

Karl shifted slightly uncomfortably. "Well, as I said, it's the sort of humour that women wouldn't find amusing. But I ain't gonna lie and say I don't laugh my balls off at Dice Man's jokes. I find the guy funny, but I know he ain't on any politically correct tip."

He could sense the possibility of an impending argument, and that was not somewhere he wanted to go right now. As Angela summoned her thoughts together to come back with a reply, Karl cut her short. Swiftly he fed her a strawberry as a way of distracting her. The sweetness of the fruit was enough to distract her from the discussion at hand. As she swallowed, Karl had already prepared another strawberry. This time he held it in his mouth and brought it closer to hers. Angela bit softly into the ripe berry as Karl held it in his mouth. Slowly she nibbled away until their lips were touching, and then she felt Karl's tongue exploring the domain of her mouth. She reciprocated, and felt the warmth of his tongue against her own. Gradually the slow and sensual exchange grew in passionate intensity until they were both frantically kissing, long and hard.

Angela could hear his breath becoming harder, and sensed his growing arousal. It made her feel horny, and before she could think further she found herself pushing Karl on to his back before lying on top of him.

She ran her fingers over his firm chest as she pushed her tongue deep into his mouth. She stopped only briefly to remove her leather jacket, which she rapidly discarded on the grass. She felt the heat of the afternoon sun glowing on her back as Karl pulled up her white T-shirt. A very light breeze was blowing, which felt pleasant against her exposed skin. As she felt his hands start to unclip her bra-strap, she figured that Karl was on a mission that afternoon. She hesitated for a moment, wondering if he was going to be able to work out the method of unfastening. But, like an old pro, Karl had unclasped her garment within seconds.

Now, from the front, he pulled up the T-shirt and bra to allow her breasts to be freed from their confinement. She felt her nipples harden as they became exposed and brushed against the leather of his motor-cycle jacket. She raised herself up just enough for the tips of her nipples to lightly touch the sensual feel of the material. Backwards and forwards she jiggled her breasts, arousing herself through the tingling running through the tips of her nipples.

Karl had noticed the growing arousal in Angela, and it sent him into a growing state of excitement. Suddenly a shiver ran down Angela's spine as she felt his hot tongue lick her left nipple. The feeling grew in intensity as his tongue's movements grew in vigour. Now he was sucking gently on her breast, softly pulling it into his mouth. Angela could feel her nipples increase still further in hardness. Now his mouth was working on her right breast. Sucking, gently biting, teasing the nipple to growing heights of firmness. His tongue circled slowly before he gently bit the firm flesh of her breast.

It was driving her wild with excitement, and Angela could feel her panties becoming increasingly wet from her pussy's desire. Her mind was a mass of excited thoughts and emotions. Her back tingled as the afternoon breeze blew on to her skin. Added to the heat of the sun, it provided a delightful cocktail of pleasure. Her vagina ached with desire, and Angela desperately wanted him to touch her, to suck her, to feel his penis inside her. But at that moment she felt too shy to ask him.

Maybe Karl was a mind-reader after all. He told her he needed to stand up, and now here he was, removing his jacket, then his black leather boots and jeans. He stood there in his Calvin Klein boxer shorts, his erect penis obviously visible through the tight confines of the grey Lycra.

Angela tried unsuccessfully to stifle a nervous laugh. "Suppose someone comes along?"

Karl was unconcerned about that possibility, and busied himself with the removal of a car blanket from the motor cycle's pannier. After unfolding it and spreading it carefully on the soft forest floor, he gesticulated for Angela to make herself comfortable on it. "No one's gonna come here at this time of the day. Relax. Anyhow, so what if they do?"

It was a question that Angela didn't have an answer for at that particular moment. And besides, her pussy had ideas of its own. Men frequently come out with that cliché about women "gagging for it", but in this case it was more than apt. But modesty is a strange bedfellow. For although Angela longed to tear off her clothes and romp naked with this handsome, muscular stud, an inbuilt reserve prevented her from doing exactly what she felt like.

Her inner turmoil was once again resolved for her by outside forces. Karl's hands reached for the top button of her jeans before moving to the zip. She made her contribution by kicking off her brown suede Nikes and lifting her bottom off the ground as he pulled her jeans down her legs. His directness and forcefulness were appealing to her, and her excitement grew at the way he pulled off her T-shirt and bra.

She wasn't too sure if she wanted to relinquish control of her panties or not. It was her last 'line of defence' against total exposure, and as Karl's fingers moved up her thigh, nearer to her underwear, she instinctively closed her legs.

Karl read the move correctly and realised that he'd need to work her into the mood. His right hand's forefinger slowly ran across the wet patch at the front of her panties, and Angela felt herself relaxing to his touch. His finger probed slightly more firmly, and she felt her clitoris harden as his fingertip toyed with it.

"Whoa, girl! From how wet you are I'd guess that you're enjoying this."

Angela exhaled deeply and pushed her mound harder against Karl's hand. His palm acted as a fine stimulator for her clitoris, and Angela made sure that his hand was put to good use. The great outdoors certainly helped the juices to flow, thought Angela as she writhed in ecstasy. She lay back and gazed up, beyond the overhanging branches of the nearby oak tree and high up into the bright blue, cloudless sky. She closed her eyes and let the warm afternoon breeze blow across her erect nipples. The sun radiated its warmth across her body and the nearby chorus of birdsong was like hypnotic music to her ears. She felt the hot breath of his mouth and his lips gently kissing her thighs. The kisses were travelling on a journey whose destination was fairly obvious to Angela. Inch by inch his lips moved upwards, teasing her skin. Oh, how her pussy waited desperately for his attention. It felt as if he was playing with her, getting her horny yet making sure she waited for her pleasure. As those soft, warm kisses came closer to her crotch she felt his tongue licking her inner thighs as close as was possible to her pussy. The ecstasy and the agony of it all was too much to bear. The feeling was of enjoying the moment but still waiting to reach heaven.

Fingers pulled the front of her panties to one side, exposing her pussy to the summer's day. Her fists clenched hard as a deep moan sprang forth. His tongue slipped past her lips and deep inside her vagina, where it probed and tickled her wetness. She gently pushed his head away to enable her to remove her panties totally. Now she was free and without any defence. It was time to relax and get horny, so she stretched herself out and opened her legs wide. Once again his tongue found its way into her cunt, where it sought out the areas of greatest pleasure. In and out of her pussy it darted, fucking her as if it were a small penis. The sensual slurping sound was like sweet music to her ears.

"Oh fuck, that feels so good," she quietly whispered. His tongue was now working at a faster rate, slapping backwards and forwards deep into her pussy. She was so moist she could feel her wetness running down her crotch and in between her buttocks. It felt like Niagara Falls, but a whole heap more exciting.

Oh yes, she thought. This guy knows how to lick pussy. Oh, you're doing that good. That's it — just there. Oh yes, oh yes, just like that. Please don't move from there. Let me just get into this feeling. . . Oh damn! He's changed the stroke. But, then again, that feels good too. . .

These innermost thoughts she would have liked to say out loud, but there are certain things that are best kept inside.

Karl lifted up her legs and let them hang over on to his back. Now, as he buried his head into her crotch and probed deep into her vagina with his tongue, her legs gripped his back, pushing her cunt upwards, hard against his mouth. His back provided the perfect support to enable Angela to writhe and shake her vagina in his face. With his face motionless and his tongue well extended, Angela pulled and pushed her pussy backwards and forwards on his tongue. Only occasionally did she break the rhythm to afford herself the pleasure of pushing herself hard against his mouth and savour the feeling of his lip pushed tight on her clitoris.

Any inhibitions she might have had were all but gone now, as she revelled in the pleasure her pussy was receiving. It was a joyous thing to meet a man who could lick pussy so well. It was a good thing to meet a man who didn't think entirely of his own pleasure but also his partner's.

Karl now expertly parted her vagina's lips with the fingers of his left hand, exposing her. Softly he blew on her clitoris, which sent shivers along her spine right into her head. Her button tingled and hardened, and when his tongue's tip licked it she thought it would explode. It was so very hard that she had to touch it to confirm for herself.

Running her finger across it made her positively throb with pleasure.

Her legs were tiring, so she slipped down on to her back again and made herself more comfortable. Karl continued his sensual onslaught on her pussy until she could feel the release of energy about to begin. She was at the very pinnacle when Karl stopped. It was as if he knew the exact moment that she was going to orgasm and decided she should wait. Angela kept her eyes closed tightly, enjoying the sensation of not being able to see yet feeling the warmth of the sun, the soft blowing of the breeze; the sounds of summer were so clear to her she didn't need to see.

"Ohhh!" A loud moan of pleasure came forth from her as he pushed the head of his penis into the mouth of her vagina. It felt hard, hot and thick inside her. Even the copious amounts of lubrication coming from her pussy still made it feel a tight fit. But as he slowly worked his cock in and out of her, it glided more easily.

Angela spread her legs wider and reached down to open her vagina to accommodate his large, fat cock. She could feel the veins standing up along his shaft. As he slowly slid his erect member into her, she felt her heart beating faster and she gasped for breath. His cock felt wickedly hard and long, and she wondered again if she could accommodate it all.

"Fuck me harder. Oh, that big dick feels so good in my pussy."

"Yeah, yeah. You like my cock in your cunt?" His voice was deep and breathless with excitement. He happily obliged the request and fucked her pussy with greater vigour.

"Oh, yes! Yes! Fuck me! Fuck me! Ohh!" Angela had reached the point of no return, and could feel the waves of an orgasmic sea crash down upon her. She groaned loud, and let out a resonating scream as she climaxed. In her moment of orgasmic quivering she felt Karl's pelvis start to shake then felt his penis pulled from inside her. It felt like warm soup as his sperm shot over her breasts and mouth. She licked her lips to taste his spunk. Thick and slightly salty was her verdict. It was all rather new to her, as she had never had anyone come in her mouth before. She'd always been curious, but had not been bold enough ever to suggest it to anyone — especially not her husband.

Karl slumped down next to her, catching his breath. He blew a long, slow, deliberate breath and groaned in pleasure.

Angela lay still, her eyes closed. Her mind wandered to all manner of diverse corners. Graffiti in the college toilets: After sucking I like fucking. She wondered if it described the writer's order of preference, or whether after one act he or she liked to perform the next as a way of coming back to earth after a good bout of sex.

Her wanderings were cut short by the sudden absence of sunlight on her face. She opened her eyes to see how big the cloud was. There, silhouetted against the afternoon sun, was the outline of a man a few yards away, staring down at them.

CHAPTER 12

I really am beginning to wonder how on earth I got involved in all of this. I know I was bored, but now I wonder if things have gone too far — or, more importantly, if I'll be able to settle back to the routine of life when Malcolm returns. I'm not sure whether I'll feel guilty when I see him, but at the moment I don't feel that way about the things I've done with Karl.

They say that at least once in a lifetime every woman deserves an adventure. Well, I guess that this is mine. It has been the most amazing fourteen days of my life. I've been to so many new places and done so many different things. I'd never been on a motor cycle before, and now I'm hooked. What a buzz. In fact the whole crazy thing is one big buzz.

I've done things with this guy that I couldn't even tell Malcolm as a fantasy thought. Karl is one of those rare black men who will try anything sexually. He's confident enough that he doesn't need to think about his image or try to live up to some macho stereotype. He's honest and straightforward in his approach to sex. He says he loves sex and it's an important part of his life. And, boy, does he love sex! I've never met any man who is so into fucking. He lives, drinks, breathes and sleeps punnany. If he's not actually doing it then he's reading about it or watching some porn video.

He's a very exciting lover and I never know what will happen next. This turns me on and scares me slightly. I never know where Karl's limits are and what he wouldn't do. I wouldn't put anything past him, and I sometimes think that he might just be the sort of person who could get into serious mind games. The sort of guy who could really fuck up your head. I'm enjoying the ride, but I'm also maintaining just enough caution. I'm being careful to see this for exactly what it is: a fun adventure that will be short lived. Karl is too much of a player around town for me to take him seriously. But that's fine — at least he is honest about it.

I have really had to rethink my own perceptions about who I am. Well, especially after last night. I still can't believe it even now, in the cold light of day. Somehow I still can't believe it was me, yet I know it was, and can see myself as clear as day.

It was another fantastic summer Friday evening and I was going to meet Karl up in Walthamstow. It was such a nice evening that I spent an hour beforehand just cruising around in the car with the hood down. London is such a cool place to be when the sun is shining. I cruised around the trendy streets of Camden and watched people hanging outside the cafes and bars. The place was absolutely teeming with people.

Then I drove over to Tottenham, and at every traffic light got chatted up by the guy in the car next to me. It was all harmless good-natured stuff, but I do wish they could be a little more imaginative with their chat-up lines. There must be something very powerful about sunshine. It brings everyone out of their shells and seems to make the world such a different place. I wonder what England would be like if the sun always shone. . .

I eventually reached Walthamstow at around 7.30 and met Karl outside the tube station. It was strange not to see him on his motor bike. The two seem so linked. But tonight we'd agreed that I'd bring the car and he'd come on the subway.

He seemed a bit moody at first. Didn't want to talk very much at all. I thought there was something troubling him, but he just said there wasn't a problem so I thought it best not to push the matter.

I'd felt in a bit of a mood myself earlier on in the day, but I didn't let it get to me. Got another strange call on the answering machine. I would like to find out who is doing this, but I'm not even sure if it's meant for me or Malcolm, or even if they've got us mixed up with someone else. It's worrying how you can get used to anything, but I must admit that I'm not as frightened about the whole thing as I was at the beginning. It makes you realise how you can get used to anything. It's frightening really.

As the evening wore on, Karl was back to his usual self so I still have no idea what was on his mind. But then again I think he is that sort of person. Keeps a lot to himself and doesn't communicate unless he thinks it's important that you need to know. I don't think he's a dishonest person, but I would have to admit that I find it difficult to come up with an assessment as to exactly what he's like as a person. It's strange how you can do the most intimate physical acts with someone, yet at the same time know nothing about what they're really like. Who is Karl Hendricks? I have to admit that I really don't know. Is he the sort of person who could murder? I don't know. Does he worry about getting old? Does he have any deep-seated fears? Does he like women? Does he have any children? What makes him laugh? There are so many questions I could ask and have no idea as to what the answers are, or even what they are likely to be.

Maybe he feels the same. Maybe he asks himself similar questions. I wonder if he asks himself, Why is this woman sleeping with me? What does she want from me? The strange thing is that he's never asked. Why? If I was a man in his position I would ask the question if for no other reason than to have my ego massaged. Yet it seems like it doesn't bother him and yet he's also quite an egotistical person.

Like I said, I really don't know him at all.

We went to Walthamstow Dog Stadium to see greyhound racing. It was so much fun. I must admit that when he suggested it I thought he was taking the piss. But it was so exciting, especially as we bet on every race. Shame we lost every bet, but as they say, you win some, you lose some. The atmosphere at the venue was truly electric. It's obviously quite an East End tradition judging by the number of people there and how seriously they took the racing. We sat outside in the stalls and had a drink, and cheeky Karl even rolled up a spliff. The funny thing was that, once he started smoking it, it was funny how many other people seemed to be smoking cigarettes with strange smells. The time passed very quickly as we cheered the dogs home, albeit from a position somewhere close to the back.

Malcolm would have laughed if he knew I'd gone dog racing. It really wouldn't be his thing at all. A night out at the theatre, maybe, but dog racing is a little bit down-market for him. But as Karl says, "Don't knock it till you've tried it."

I tried finding out about what he does for a living, but as ever he was very vague about it.

"People in this country are obsessed with how people make money. They are too wrapped up with foolishness about how big their car is or where they live. Status is the killer of creativity and individuality," was what he actually said. I don't know if he really believes that, or whether he thinks it's cool to be like that. Part of me thinks that Karl is as wrapped up with the whole material bullshit as everyone else but he just doesn't want to admit it. He likes the idea of being a free thinker and an individual too much to be compared to Mister Average in the high street.

Blue Boy nearly won, but at the last corner he slipped and the pack rushed past him. It was the closest I got to picking a winner

133

that night, and I felt my disappointment being carried on to Blue Boy's shoulders. I could see from the dejected way he strolled back to his handler that he knew he'd messed up big-time. I hope he got a good beating that night for making me lose my £1 bet (JOKE!).

I felt quite tipsy sitting in the evening sunshine drinking 'nuff glasses of wine. I don't know how many I had, because I was a bit distracted by the whole spectacle of the event. Karl kept buying drinks And I kept drinking them. I must have forgotten that I was the one who was supposed to be driving. I told Karl that I wasn't in any state to drive and that we should take a cab, but he just told me I was being foolish and that I worried too much. But then that's typical of him. He enjoys taking risks and expects the same of others. I think I'm too old to be pulling stunts, but it's his life if he wants to live it that way. I thought we were going to get into an argument, but fortunately he backed down and said he would drive. He claimed he'd not drunk more that two halves of beer and, as I hadn't seen him having any more than that, I accepted his word.

That business yesterday at the woods just freaked me out. I have never been so embarrassed in my life. When I opened my eyes and saw that man there I could have died. Karl just styled it out. Thank God. I thought that he might have attacked the man.

Karl casually got up and put on his trousers and lit a cigarette. He asked the guy if he'd "enjoyed the show". But when the man started speaking we could tell that he wasn't all there in the head. A 'Simple Simon', as my mother would say. It made it all the more embarrassing. I don't think he had a clue what was going on and was obviously fascinated about two people having sex. It was all very creepy and I think it's removed my interest in sex in the great outdoors. That's the trouble with Britain. There are too many people here to have sex without someone disturbing you.

Karl said some strange things to this guy, which made me wonder at the time. He asked the guy, if he stabbed him, would anyone miss him? I think he was just being a bit macho to cover his embarrassment at literally being caught with his pants down.

Anyway, near argument avoided, we decided to go to a club in the West End that Karl sometimes frequents. Mars was packed with lots of very trendy and beautiful people. Hip, creative types with obviously a lot of disposable income. Poor old Malcolm would have felt totally out of place there, and I have to admit that I did feel a little bit too square for the trendies.

Mars is very modern and stylish, and the owner has obviously spent a whole heap of money on the venue. From the number of bottles of champagne I saw being bought, he obviously attracts the type of crowd who spend enough money to justify his investment.

If there's soul playing I'm dancing, so me and Karl quickly go into the groove. As I wasn't driving I thought I might as well not worry about drinking, so I didn't. While we were dancing a tall, blonde woman came over to Karl and starting chatting about something, but it was too loud for me to hear. Later on he introduced her as Stacey. He had apparently met her at the club before, but when she went to the toilet he admitted that he couldn't remember her.

I was a bit defensive towards her at first. I thought it was a bit feisty of her just to start chatting to the man I was with. But she turned out to be a nice person, and as the evening wore on we started to get on really well. She worked for a major film company in Soho, and I could tell from her upper-class accent that she wasn't born on the wrong side of the tracks. She lives southside, down in Battersea, so Karl offered her a lift home. We left around 3.00 a.m., and in what seemed like just a few minutes we were outside her flat. She asked us in for something to eat as

135

Karl was starving. We ate chicken salad sandwiches in her kitchen and reflected on what had been the best moments of our lives. Stacey is thirty-three, and I asked her why she lives alone. Said she was a confirmed "bachelorette", and wanted to remain that way. I could understand her reasoning. She's obviously enjoying life that way. She has a good job, a stunning flat, money, and is in great shape. In fact she looked much younger than her years. (Unusual for blondes, who seem to age quickly. The price you pay for having more fun, I guess!)

She works out a lot, which has inspired me to go to the gym more regularly. (Must make a note and put it on fridge door.) She really had a figure that many women would have died for, but then again every other woman's figure always seems to look better than your own. (Why are we women always so concerned about our figures? Why do men make so little effort with theirs?)

We retired to the lounge and had a glass of wine. Stacey got out her little tin and Karl rolled a couple of rather generous spliffs. (Why do men always roll bigger spliffs when they're using someone else's weed?) I can't say I'm much of a spliff-smoker, but I did try some last night. I coughed at first, but I think I got into it after a while. (Is this how you're supposed to feel?)

Then out of the blue Karl says to Stacey, "What do you think of Angela? Do you think she's sexy?"

Stacey blushed and smiled and looked in every direction but at us. Then Karl repeats the question and says he wants an answer. Well, Stacey gives me a quick glance to see my reaction. And at this point I'm just curious to know her answer. She smiles and says, "Yes, I do think Angela is sexy."

"You know why I asked that question?" said Karl, without giving her a chance to answer. "Because I've noticed the way you've been looking at Angela's tits and pussy all night."

Now I'm beginning to feel embarrassed, but at the same time I'm very intrigued about what Karl is saying and Stacey's reaction. It was like the ultimate truth-or-dare game. Karl was getting himself in a position where he was controlling the moment and I could see that he was enjoying that. I could also see that, despite her embarrassment, Stacey was also getting off on it. I felt more of an observer, but at the same time I felt more and more drawn into the mind-games.

Karl wasn't letting up for a moment. "You see, Stacey, I noticed you doing that when you thought Angela wasn't looking. Am I telling the truth?"

Poor Stacey blushed a deeper shade of crimson and kept smiling and looking at the floor.

"Am I telling the truth, Stacey?" He was not going to give up on this line of questioning.

Then Stacey looked straight at him as if I wasn't there and said, "Yes."

I have to admit that I felt very flattered and on a bit of an ego trip. I enjoyed seeing her embarrassment and I hoped Karl would keep pumping her.

True to form, he didn't disappoint me. "So, would you like to fuck Angela?" he asked.

Stacey was obviously lowering her guard, because this time there was no hesitation. She looked at him in a very submissive way and quietly said, "Yes."

I've never had a sexual relationship with another woman, but I've always been curious. Hearing another woman speak about me in this way was both quite shocking and a big turn-on at the same time. I felt my heart start to beat faster and I sensed my pussy get a little wet.

"Okay, Stacey, what I think you should do is to get down on your knees and move over to Angela and ask her if you could look at her tits."

At that moment I wondered if this was all a set-up and that the two of them had done this before. Karl seemed very confident of himself to speak to someone he didn't really know like that. I thought she would tell him to get out, but she didn't. She did exactly as he told her and came over to me on her knees and asked the question. Maybe in other circumstances I would have thought Karl's male power trip out of order, but I actually got very turned on by the whole thing. I don't know why, but I did. Maybe deep in my subconscious I enjoyed seeing this woman being dominated because she was white. I think there are probably a lot of subconscious things that go on in many sexual experiences.

Well, if Stacey was playing Karl's game, I was as guilty of doing the same. I found myself lifting up my white shirt and bra and letting her look at my breasts. I felt like a total exhibitionist but I enjoyed doing it.

"Stacey, would you like to see Angela's pussy?"

Dutifully, Stacey nodded her head and asked me, "Angela, may I please look at your fanny?"

By this point I thought, What the hell, she did say "please". . . I pulled down my brown ski-pants and gave her a look at my bush. She sat on the sofa next to me and pulled up her black party dress to reveal that she wasn't wearing any panties. She had really long pubic hair, but it looked like it had been brushed and blow-dried, it was so groomed. It reminded me of something from a fairy story. Rapunzel and her Golden Minge, maybe. I was curious to see what it felt like, especially as I always like to keep mine very short and trimmed. I always used to think there was something unfeminine about having too much hair down there.

"Mary, Mary, quite contrary, trim that bush it's so damn hairy" was a rhyme the boys at a nearby comprehensive used to sing to us passing schoolgirls. So maybe it's not just me. . .

Stacey started to rub her clitoris with her fingers. I was shocked and fascinated at the same time. It was all so new and exciting that I didn't know what I should be doing. I looked across at Karl, but he seemed to be elsewhere; he was smoking a spliff and staring out of the window in deep contemplation about something. A moment later he went out of the lounge and I could hear him rummaging through the fridge. I felt slightly more relaxed with him out of the way, as I felt there would not be anyone looking at me in judgement. Not that Karl is like that. He's the kinkiest person I know.

Stacey stopped her display of masturbation and started to unbutton my shirt before removing both that and my bra. I offered no resistance. She stood and slipped her dress over her head. With her slim, small, upturned breasts with large nipples, Stacey looked very different without her clothes. (What did I expect her to look like?) She sat back on the sofa and continued playing with herself. In a slow and deliberate way she slipped a finger into her pussy, withdrew it, then advanced her hand towards my right breast. Her fingertip extended and she lubricated my nipple with her juice. I don't know how much of it was to do with arousal or the shock of the new, but I felt myself shaking with excitement. My heart beat faster and I visibly shivered.

The immediate impression was of how soft her finger felt. Men's hands are so much rougher, that the difference was very noticeable. Now she was softly squeezing my nipple between her finger and thumb, making it feel hard and warm. It felt fantastic, and the more she did it the better it felt. She brought her mouth to my breast and suckled my nipple as if she were a small child. At that moment any resistance I might have had to making love to a woman disappeared. It felt so very sexy, and all I could think about was what it would be like to put my mouth to her pussy. I wondered how it would feel to taste another woman; at last I could discover how it felt to be a man going down on a woman. The thought kept going through my mind.

My hand reached to her pussy. Her bush was soft but moist from her juices. I played for a while with her hair, savouring the feel of it in my fingers. Very soft, I kept thinking. My finger found her clitoris and gently my fingertip explored and excited it. I felt it slowly harden to my touch, which was quite a turn on. Stacey let out a deep sigh as my finger made its way into her vagina. Liberal amounts of her wetness ran over my hand as I gently worked in and out of her.

"Harder," she moaned, grabbing my hand and pushing it into her pussy. I happily obliged, easing my finger into her with increased vigour. Occasionally I would stop to touch her clitoris to settle my curiosity about its firmness.

She again made a request. This time she asked me to insert another finger. And again I was happy to be of assistance. After a short while she pulled my fingers from her wetness and proceeded to remove my shoes and my remaining items of clothing.

With me sprawled back on the sofa, my legs slightly apart, Stacey took her opportunity to go directly to my pussy. The directness of her approach gave me quite a shudder as she thrust her tongue straight inside me. It was shockingly pleasurable as her tongue probed deeper. It licked the walls of my vagina, giving me one of the most indescribable feelings of pleasure I have ever encountered. The softness of a woman's skin next to my vagina was a new and very different experience, but I was also struck by the fact of how similar it felt to a man doing it. For some reason

I had imagined that the sensation would have been completely different but it was not a million light years away.

I was getting so wet it was almost embarrassing. How strange to have another woman licking me out, I thought. But, oh, how it made me shiver with excitement. She licked and gently sucked my clitoris so much that at one point I thought I was going to come. She seemed to know exactly where and how to touch me with her fingers and tongue.

My hands found her breasts and I couldn't resist playing with her nipples, feeling them stiffen to my touch. Incredibly long, they just seemed to get bigger and bigger the more I fondled them.

I lay back and watched Stacey on her knees, bottom in the air, face in my pussy, licking me to new heights of ecstasy. I closed my eyes and let my pussy enjoy all the stimulation it could handle. 'Glorious' is the only word I can think of to describe the feeling. Absolutely glorious. Pure niceness, as June would probably call it. Oh, that Stacey sucks pussy really very well. Now, if all men could do it this way, half the world's population would be walking around with a permanent smile.

I opened my eyes when I heard Karl coming back into the lounge. He was stark naked, carrying an opened bottle of champagne. His big erection bounced in front of him like the horn of a rhino and he had the biggest grin on his face. "Good to see you girls are getting to know each other."

Stacey ignored him and carried on licking my cunt. At this point I was so relaxed that his arrival didn't make me feel reserved. In fact it sexed me up quite a bit to see his dick get harder as he watched us on the sofa.

He swigged from the bottle, playing it cool. But I knew it would not be long before he couldn't resist joining in the fun and games.

Sure enough, after a few minutes he was walking over to the settee. His hands squeezed Stacey's bottom before he slipped his fingers between her legs and started to work her pussy from behind. A moment later I watched as he guided his large ebony-coloured penis into the pinkness of her flesh.

I felt a gasp of hot air come from her mouth as he entered her from behind.

His large hands gripped her bottom as his pelvis moved with a rhythm that was beautiful to watch. Stacey licked me with greater excitement as her pussy received the attention it so craved. Karl's eyes and mine made contact, and for a while we stared at each other, both of us showing each other the amount of pleasure we were receiving. Karl's face was slightly contorted with the stimulation his cock was getting, and small beads of sweat were forming at his temples. It was like so many things that evening — a total mind-blowing turn-on to see his face as he fucked her pussy.

He looked at me and mouthed the words: "You rude bitch."

In turn I looked him in the eye and told him what a "dirty bastard" he was. We both smiled at each other, understanding exactly how the other was feeling.

Karl had brought his right hand round to the front of Stacey's pussy and was busy stimulating her clitoris. I could hear her breathing heavily and I could feel her arousal as if it were mine also.

Her excitement became more vocal and in what seemed like a very short time she was moaning loudly as she orgasmed.

While Stacey caught her breath on the sofa, me and Karl got busy on the lounge carpet. I was in need of some cock myself, and made my desire very clear to Karl. He lay outstretched on the floor while I carefully positioned myself over his penis. With my right hand firmly gripping his shaft and my left opening the lips of my pussy, I carefully guided his ting into me. It felt as hard as rock and was so swollen that it was with some difficulty that I took it.

His cock was too much for my pussy, so I had to avoid taking it all into me. But as my vagina acclimatised itself to his large member, I was able to lower myself down on him with greater confidence.

As any woman will testify, it's a lovely feeling to sit on a firm, fat cock. The sense of fulfilment and the feeling of control is very appealing. I was moving myself up and down on him, stopping only to rub my clitoris or play with my nipples. If I bent forward I could see Karl's penis inside of me, its shaft glistening in the candlelight with the juice of my pussy. I could see Stacy sitting on the sofa watching us while she toyed with her vagina.

The fun was too much for her to be excluded, and she soon joined in. Walking across to Karl, she took my lead and brought her pussy into contact with him. Facing me, she squatted over his face and lowered her pussy on to his mouth. I watched, mesmerised, as Karl pushed his tongue into her, then proceeded to lick her with a lot of enthusiasm. I could tell he was enjoying it by the way his penis flexed inside of me. By Stacey's wide-mouthed expression, it was clear that she was also having a good time. Inhibition was something that had long gone out of the window. She was moaning very loudly and calling out to Karl, saying, "Suck me, suck me."

He started to suck her clitoris and in what seemed like seconds she was having another orgasm. The girl had come twice already

143

and I was only just warming up. Whatever she was on, I wanted some of that! Oh well, it was every man (or woman) for themselves — and I wanted mine. With the palms of my hands resting on Karl's rather firm abdomen, I pushed myself up and down on his wood while Stacey helped me get there by licking my clitoris. I could feel it coming; all I needed to do was keep my mind focused and forget everything else.

Soon came the point of no return. That shiver that starts in the centre of your pussy and travels up your spine like waves. . . A deep, deep groan, and I was being washed away by one of the nicest orgasms I've had in a long time.

Suddenly his penis inside of me was too much and I had to pull myself off. I sat on the carpet feeling a bit guilty about leaving Karl in mid-stream.

"Hey, what about me?" he pleaded, half jokingly. "Typical, innit? Woman gets what she wants and she don't wanna know."

We all had a laugh, and Stacey took pity on Karl. She started sucking his penis while wanking him with her right hand. But Karl was still in a joking mood. He looked across at me and said, "Angela, didn't anyone ever tell you that two heads were better than one?"

Karl was in second heaven. Two of us sucking and licking his cock while he lay back and thought of somewhere that must have been very nice. I held his penis tightly in my hand and wanked him with long, even strokes. Stacey meanwhile sucked his head, which was having the desired effect. His cock tightened as he was about to come, and Stacey withdrew her mouth so as to witness his moment of pleasure. A long spurt of spunk shot from his dick, followed by another two or three. It came to rest on Stacey's breasts, where it ran like a small stream over her left nipple. Karl lay there, breathing heavily with a wide grin on his face.

We chilled out by rolling spliffs and drinking champagne. No one bothered to put their clothes back on, which I quite liked. I felt relaxed and, at that moment, as carefree as I've ever felt. Nothing like that had ever happened to me before and — who knows — it may never happen again.

That night I felt decadent, rude and unbelievably liberated. I had dared to open my mind and explore something that I had fantasised about but never experienced. I wonder how many people will go to their grave with a mind full of unfulfilled fantasies. How many will wish they'd had the courage to get on the plane to Istanbul, or cross the desert in that jeep, or cover their wife in chocolate sauce? We all have so many dreams and fantasies, yet we never dare think that they can ever become reality. If nothing else, I feel that little bit happier knowing that part of my curiosity has now been fulfilled. The feeling of tiresome boredom that has gripped my life over the last year or so has disappeared. This adventure is doing me so much good. The question I keep asking myself is, will it all end in tears?

CHAPTER 13

The feeling of not being bothered to go out was heavy on my mind. The only thing that I felt like doing was spending time being given all the attention that my pussy could take. Last night's activity with Stacey left me feeling like I just wanted to stay in at Karl's.

We'd got back there early Saturday morning and had spent most of the day in bed sleeping. He went out at four, saying he had to sort out something and would be about an hour, but it was not until eight that I heard his keys in the door.

Although I was dressed, I felt sure that I could persuade him that going to the party was not such a good idea.

We enjoyed a drink together and talked idly about nothing in particular. The conversation belied the need that we had for each other's bodies, but the game that we had both set out to play continued. Even though the conversation was not centred around the act of sex, I knew that I'd be given what I wanted.

We relaxed on the settee, barely touching, and as the night progressed and the alcohol flowed I felt the pressure of sexual tension rising in my body.

He was sitting at the other end of the settee with one foot casually resting on the other. The music that was playing reminded me of when I used to frequent blues parties when I was younger.

There's nothing better than the feeling of a man rubbing himself into you at a dance. The feeling of my pussy getting wet made me move my hand between my legs, and I knew that he was paying attention when I felt him start to shake one of his feet in time to the music.

Turning over on to my stomach, my fingers reached out to the hi-fi system and put on a different choice of music. Taking him by the hand I led him to a corner of the room, hesitating only to turn down the light on my way past the switch. As I pressed my back into the wall and pulled him with me I wondered which one of us had won this battle.

Moving my body in time to the music I pushed myself deliberately against his hard dick, making it obvious that I knew he had been waiting all night to get his fingers inside my wet pussy.

I could feel him trying to match my rhythm each time I changed it, and the thought of his dick being inside me made me decide that this battle was mine.

As we started to wind up against the wall with no pretence of dancing, I moved my lips up to kiss him.

I moaned into his mouth at the urgent sound made by the metal ends of his belt as they struck together. My hands met his at the buttons on his jeans, and soon they were half-way down his thighs.

He opened his legs to prevent the jeans from falling any further and leant with both hands against the wall He kissed my mouth down in the direction that he wanted me to go.

His dick looked even sexier in the 'blues' lighting. Hesitating just for a moment to take in the view, I parted my lips and took his penis deep into my mouth. I heard the deep groan that told me I had been quick to hit the spot tonight and, bearing this in mind,

I removed his shaft so that I could look at it again with its new sheen.

I used my hand to pull him back into my mouth and toyed my tongue around his dick. With my spare hand I pulled up my dress and put my hand down my knickers to feel how wet my pussy was getting.

"Do you love it?"

I moaned on to his penis as the impact of the question made my mouth quiver around his dick, and I felt my pussy gush in anticipation of the next time that he would ask it.

"Do you love it?"

Again I answered the question with a gush from my mouth.

"Oh, you do love it!" He stroked his hand through my hair and it felt like the most intimate act. As he touched he pushed his dick gently into my mouth in time to the sensual rhythm of the music.

I moved my fingers from my pussy to stop myself from coming. I needed to come on his dick. Standing up to meet his waiting mouth with mine, I pulled my knickers part way down my thighs as I guided his dick into me.

The position of my knickers on my thighs made the entry difficult, and this heightened the urgency of the moment. My shallow moans told him that I was about to come and he wanted to be there to feel it.

He pulled urgently at the front of my knickers and, failing to rip them, he pulled them back up my legs with a force that pushed me to growl his name. Pulling my knickers to one side he used his hand to work his tool into my willing cunt.

His other hand moved round to support my buttocks, and the heat from his hands was welcome after the stark coldness of the wall. Still holding his dick he withdrew from me. He rubbed my juice back into my pussy and followed it in with his dick.

This time he held my buttocks with both hands and supported my weight against the wall. His strokes were long and purposeful, and he fucked me like a man who was on a mission.

As he pumped me with robotic accuracy I allowed the full weight of my body to fall into his hands. He lifted me up until his cock was barely inside me and moved me with short sharp pulls on to his dick.

I moved my hips to try and get his full length into me, but he had already anticipated the move and swiftly lifted me away from his dick. The unexpectedness of the action excited me even more, and he noticed how his teasing made me groan louder.

"Do you want to come, baby?"

"Yes," I said.

"Beg me."

His words made my pussy gush.

"Beg me," he said again.

"Make me come."

I could feel his slow, deliberate withdrawal from my pussy, and he knew by my moan when he had hit the spot. I could feel my clit quivering as he rubbed his dick back and forth over the spot. My attention focused solely at the sensations that were about to burst through my body, and the realisation that the growling I could hear was being made by me sent me into a wave of climax.

"I love it. I love it."

We slid down to the floor with a laugh of togetherness. But each of us had our own reasons. It was the sort of. . .

The knock at the front door stopped Angela's writing mid-sentence. She collected the hand-written pages, popped them into the diary, and pulled herself off the bed.

As she opened the front door her mouth dropped.

"What are you doing here?" The words sprang from her mouth with a tone of shock and hostility that she couldn't control. "How the hell did you get my address?"

Karl didn't look best pleased by the reception. "Hey, relax. What's the problem? I was literally up the road visiting a friend, and I thought I'd pay you a surprise visit. Can we go in rather than discuss this on the doorstep?"

Angela tried to compose herself and showed Karl into the front room. He accepted her offer of coffee and dropped his helmet and leather jacket on an armchair. He walked around, surveying the room's furnishings, nodding to himself. At the fireplace he stopped and looked hard at a silver-framed photograph of Angela and her husband on their wedding day.

As Angela arrived back from the kitchen with two cups of coffee she noticed him moving quickly away from the mantelpiece. "Listen, Karl, I'm sorry I was a bit hostile a moment ago, but it was a shock to see you. Also, you know my circumstances. I mean, what. . ."

". . .Would the neighbours say!" he cut in mid-sentence.

"No, that's not what I was going to say. I was thinking if a friend or my husband was here. . ."

"But he's away on business, so what's the problem?"

"Yeah, and suppose he came back early?"

"Angela, life is full of ifs and maybes. The fact of the matter is that the man ain't here, so there's no point making it into a big deal. You've made it clear you don't want me round your yard and I hear you loud and clear."

She could hear the annoyance in his voice and decided it was time to try and defuse the situation. "I'm sorry. I don't mean to sound horrible."

"Angela, don't worry. I ain't coming here to cause any grief. As I said, I was just passing and in hindsight I shouldn't have just called round like that." Karl looked around the room again before sitting to drink his coffee. "You have a nice home. Malcolm must be doing very well for himself. Seymour, Burgess, Anderson must be doing very well these days."

Angela looked puzzled. "How did you know what my husband's firm was called? You haven't had any dealings with them, have you?"

"Oh, Angela, your memory is so short. The first time we went out you told me that. You're surprised that I remembered, aren't you? The thing is I actually listen to what people say. That's why I'm very good at remembering things."

She felt slightly embarrassed. "Sorry. I can't remember half of what I say. I think I have too much on my mind. Yes, Malcolm is doing very well. Which enables us to live in a very nice flat like this. But money isn't everything. The most important thing is that you enjoy life, and money can't guarantee that."

"True. I hear what you're saying, but as the man said, 'Money can't buy you happiness, but it sure can buy you a better standard of misery.' Unfortunately it's what makes the world go around. Check half of those brothas out on the street. They wouldn't be out there fighting the law if they had money. It's all about economics."

"Yes, I agree. But no one's going to come and hand you a bag full of cash. In this world most people have to work damn hard for what they have. I know Malcolm has. Anyway, it looks like you're doing all right for yourself too."

Karl smiled, but there was a coldness about his eyes that made Angela think it was not sincere.

"Everything is relative. I'm doing okay. But I could have done a lot better. I was a lot better than most of those wankers I used to work with in the City, but I watched them get the breaks because of the public school thing, and the fact that they didn't want to see a black man get ahead. I was better than those bastards, and they knew it."

The hostility Angela saw in Karl was a surprise, as it was a side of him that she'd not witnessed before. "But I thought you were glad to be out of working in the City. It was your decision to leave."

He smiled the same smile again, pausing to compose himself. "Yes, it was my decision — and I have no regrets, but part of the reason for my packing it all in was because of the whole workings of the system."

There was clearly a level of bitterness in Karl that was being kept close to his chest. Angela was curious to know more, but felt it was not for her to press the matter.

They sat and talked for a couple of hours about a host of different topics, but all the while Angela was acutely aware of how uncomfortable she felt with Karl sitting in her lounge. She felt nervous about him being in her married space. While she was at his house or out somewhere else, she could feel as though she was escaping from her own dull little world. It was a fantasy that could be kept away from the reality of home and husband and responsibility. Now, with him here, it brought home to her how difficult it may be to separate fantasy from reality.

For the second time that morning the front door knocker caught her by surprise.

"Oh shit, who's that?" she gulped, getting to her feet.

She crept to the bay of the front window and peered round the curtain to ascertain the identity of her unexpected caller. She'd hoped to remain hidden so she could avoid answering the door, but her ship of hope soon crashed on the rocks. The woman caller, for whatever reason, turned from the door to stare at the front window and caught sight of Angela peeping out from behind the curtain. She smiled and gave a wave. Angela forced a smile and retreated from the window.

"Oh shit!" Panic was starting to come over her. "Quick, take your jacket and helmet and go upstairs and wait in the first room on the right. Please, Karl, don't make a sound."

She waited until she could hear the upstairs bedroom door close before going to the front door.

"Hello, dear, I thought you were going to leave me on that front doorstep all day." The round-faced woman in her mid-sixties was smiling, but her annoyance at being kept waiting was clear to see.

Angela invited her in, apologising for the wait and blaming the fact that she was on the telephone.

Anthea Seymour was not one of Angela's favourite people, but with marriage not only comes a husband, but you get a mother-in-law thrown into the bargain. The problem with Mrs Seymour was that she doted on her son, and nothing and nobody was good enough for her Malcolm. In her little ways she would be critical of Angela, but it was always subtle enough to avoid an argument blowing up. Whenever she called, it made Angela imagine she was in the army and awaiting a kit inspection from the sergeant major.

"I thought I would pay you a visit and make sure you were coping all right without Malcolm." Like a hungry eagle, very little passed her attention. She looked at the two coffee cups and at the pair of black motorcycle gloves on the floor near the fireplace.

"Oh! You 'ave company, then."

Angela decided to play dumb. "Sorry?"

"I was saying you've had visitors. I noticed the two cups and did spy those motor bike gloves over there. And I saw a motor bike jus' outside your house." As ever, Mrs Seymour's tone was laced with suspicion.

"Oh, I had a plumber around earlier. He must have forgotten his gloves," Angela said, trying to sound disinterested.

"It's funny that he left his motor bike here. . ."

"Maybe he went somewhere nearby," suggested Angela, hoping that Mrs Seymour would now let the matter drop. Thankfully she did.

Angela started cleaning the kitchen to give the impression that she was busy so she would not have to engage in some long and tedious conversation with her mother-in-law. When she saw Mrs Seymour pull up a chair and make herself comfortable at the kitchen table, Angela decided it was time for something more drastic.

"Mrs Seymour, I hope you don't think I'm being rude, but I'm just about to go out so I'll need to start to get ready. You know, have a shower and so forth." It was Angela's habit to call her mother-in-law "Mrs Seymour" rather than "Mum" or by her first name. She had always done so, and as the woman clearly disliked her daughter-in-law it seemed right to Angela that she should continue the formality.

Mrs Seymour sounded rather put out. "Oh, well, thats no problem. I only called on the off chance, but you obviously have tings to do. I'll say my goodbyes, then." Mrs Seymour picked up her handbag and it was with great relief that Angela waved her goodbye and closed the front door behind her.

She leaned back on the hallway wall and exhaled in relief. Her heart had been beating nineteen to the dozen while Mrs Seymour did her detective work, and it was a stressful ordeal she didn't want to repeat in a hurry.

"Yo! Is it safe to come out now? Or do I have to spend the rest of the afternoon shut in this wardrobe?"

CHAPTER 14

Greenbridge Street was very quiet now. At one o'clock in the morning most of the inhabitants of the up-market St John's Wood neighbourhood had retired to bed after the usual trauma of getting back to work on Monday after an active weekend. For Angela Seymour it would have been time that she was soundly tucked up in bed, but on this warm summer's night she was finding it difficult to sleep.

The house was in darkness apart from the illumination of the full moon that burst forth through the open windows of her bedroom. She walked the confines of her room like a caged lioness seeking something that would rest her soul. She was in good spirits, but not able to settle for the night. She was tired after the weekend, yet not enough to fall asleep.

Maybe it was the conversation she'd had earlier on the phone with her brother Cliff that had made her so lively. Clifford, who was the eldest of the siblings, lived in Bristol and worked for a major food distributor. He was the funniest person Angela knew, and had been on form during their two-hour-long conversation. She'd been still laughing to herself long after they'd said goodbye.

She stood by the window now, and tried to catch whatever cool breeze the hot night might have to offer. The length and breadth of the street was in darkness. Was there no one who wanted to stay up late on a Monday night? she asked herself.

She wasn't sure how long she had been standing there daydreaming, but the clumping sound of shoes on the pavement broke her self-induced spell. She noticed that the youth, dressed in blue jeans and a hooded sweatshirt top, was keeping his head down with his eyes focused on the ground. He looked suspicious, and Angela wondered what car he was going to pick on. When he stopped by her Golf and started to peer through the window she felt a rage build up inside her. She was still wearing her day clothes, so it was just a case of pulling on some training shoes before she was down the stairs and quietly opening the front door.

As she crept out the door she could see across the road the small hooded figure of the youngster duck down beside the car. Now, as she stealthily crossed the road, she could hear the unmistakable hiss of air escaping from a car's tyre. She was now absolutely fuming with rage.

As she approached the side of the car and came round to the other side from the front, she saw the vandal about to push a small screwdriver into the tyre's side.

Her yell of "Oi!" was loud enough to wake the dead, and so startled the youth that he dropped the screwdriver and jumped to his feet. He'd got maybe a few yards before a furious Angela had charged and pushed him from behind, sending him crashing to the ground. The youngster fell face-down into the pavement, hitting his head with such force that it knocked any fight he may have had straight out of him.

"What the hell do you think you're doing?" Angela barked at the back of his head. Grabbing his shoulder, she rolled him on to his back to continue the verbal onslaught.

At that precise moment she couldn't believe her eyes. The facial features were those of a woman, not a man. Then, as she looked closer, a horrible realisation came to her. But it was too shocking to believe. She pulled away the hood and stared in disbelief.

"I'm sorry, I'm sorry," blurted the woman. "I was just so desperate."

Angela was lost for words. She could not understand what it was all about, and simply didn't know what to say or do. "Why? What the hell is all this about?"

Before the woman could speak, Angela pulled her to her feet and proceeded to frogmarch her across the road to her front door. "You're gonna sit down and explain what the raas is going down!"

Angela's rage had been tempered by the shock, and now she was determined to get to the truth. The vandal was escorted through the front door and instructed to take a seat in the lounge. Angela stood by the fireplace, arms crossed, about to start her interrogation.

"I just can't believe this, Karen. What have I done to you to deserve this. I. . ." Angela thought for a moment. "It was obviously you who sent that disgusting thing in the post, and it's you who's been making those phone calls. It's you, isn't it? Don't just fucking sit there like you don't know what I'm talking about. It was you, wasn't it?"

Karen stared at her lap, saying nothing.

"I'm asking you a question, Karen!"

Meekly Karen nodded her head in agreement.

"You fucking bitch! I should call the police. . . and you're going to sort out getting my car fixed first thing tomorrow morning."

Angela paced up and down the lounge trying to contain her fury and trying to make sense of it all. She felt betrayed, confused, angry, and a half-dozen other emotions thrown into the bargain. Fists clenched by her side, she paced for a few moments more, gathering her thoughts together. "To think that I sat with you, telling you what had happened to me, and you acted liked you were concerned. You even had the bloody feistiness to try and blame someone else! I should knock your fucking rahtid head off. You little two-faced, devious bitch, you!"

She paused, took a deep breath. "Okay, so what have I done to you, Karen?"

Karen remained silent.

"Don't look at the floor, Karen — just tell me what the hell all these fuckries are about!"

The power of anger can do amazing things to someone's personality. Angela was not the sort of person given to losing her temper, but now, as a wave of fury washed through her, she was finding reserves of aggression and assertiveness that she very rarely called upon. It was not a side that Karen had witnessed before, and it made her frightened. She sat on the sofa, her face highlighted by the large, red bruise on her forehead that seemed to grow more unpleasant looking by the minute. She wanted the ground to swallow her up at that moment, but she knew that there was no escape. She would have to sit and take her medicine. Still, she was hoping that by

159

remaining silent she could avoid having to discuss the matter any further, but she did not reckon on a woman who was so determined to resolve the matter.

Angela could take it no more. Grabbing a poker from the antique brass coal-scuttle by the fireplace, she stormed over to Karen who held her hands to her head in fear.

Angela raised her right hand and held the poker as if it were a sword. "You'd better starting talking, Karen, or I swear to God I don't know what the hell I might end up doing this night. Girl, you better start talking to me."

The look of fear was clear in Karen's eyes. She pressed herself into the sofa, fearing that at any moment a barrage of blows from the wicked-looking poker would start to rain down on her head. Finally she spoke. "I didn't want to do it, but Karl told me to. I swear I don't know why. I asked him but he wouldn't tell me."

Angela sat down on the sofa, shocked for the second time that night.

For the next two hours Karen told the whole story of her involvement with Karl Hendricks. She had met him over five years ago and had become totally obsessed with him. But to him the affair was no more than a sexual dalliance and he'd soon grown bored of the possessive Karen. She was devastated when he told her it was over, and took an overdose. Over the years she'd come to realise that nothing she did would win over his affection. But despite knowing this, she had not been able to break away. She was under his spell and there was nothing she could do about it. She could rationally tell herself that it was madness, but still she was powerless. He'd used her when he felt like it, and during the years she had allowed herself to be humiliated and abused by him. His latest request had been to start to frighten her own friend by way of threatening telephone calls and unpleasant packages and letters. He had suggested a week ago to start to do things like slash her car tyres. She said she had no idea why he wanted her to do these things. But he had told her to do it, and part of her was glad to do it — out of jealousy over Angela's present involvement with him. He had told Karen from the beginning that his plan was to have an affair with Angela. It had seemed more like a mission than an action born out of lust, but he'd refused to discuss it with her. He'd simply said what he wanted her to do and she had agreed to do as she was asked.

Angela sat and listened intently to what Karen told her while trying to work out what course of action she should take. If what the woman was saying was correct, something more sinister lay behind this whole thing. But how could she trust Karen? How did she know that this woman was telling her the truth? Was this all a pack of lies to put her off Karl? She just didn't know what to think, mainly because none of it seemed to make any sense. Why would Karl Hendricks have anything against her? She had never met the man before in her life, yet if Karen was to be believed this whole plot had been instigated before the relationship had even begun. . .

When she was convinced that there was no more that Karen knew or was willing to divulge, Angela told her to leave. But before that she warned Karen of one thing: "If you mention a thing about what has happened tonight to Karl or anyone else, I will go straight to the police. I hear the courts are coming down very rough on people who are convicted of stalking."

After Karen had gone, Angela knew it would be practically impossible for her to get any sleep. It was past three o'clock already, and in theory she had things to sort out first thing tomorrow. At least college had broken up so she didn't need to go in, she thought to herself.

She poured herself a large brandy and retired to her bedroom. It was somehow always easier to think while lying on her bed, and if she did manage to drop off she, at least, was in the right location. But her reasonings seemed to be going nowhere. She couldn't think what to do, because none of it made any sense. If she knew that Karen's story was bona fide, at least that would be a starting point. But a starting point to what? She would still be none the wiser as to why Karl would want to frighten her. He had come across as being a fairly honest guy. This all seemed so strange.

She thought about confronting him directly, but then thought it through. If he was guilty he would deny it all, and if he was innocent he would do the same. It was a no-win situation. But she would need answers quickly, as the last thing she needed was her husband returning in the middle of some psychological terror game.

Angela was due to meet up with Karl tomorrow evening, and she wondered how the hell she would be able to play it cool. Was she in danger? How close was the grand finale? She had no choice but to play along with it while covering her back. It was a dangerous game, she told herself, but what choice did she have?

CHAPTER 15

Throughout the entire journey to Wandsworth Angela had been shaking with nerves. Now, as she pulled up outside Karl's house, she desperately tried to compose herself. She sat in the car trying to rid herself of the nervousness which would alert him.

"Relax. Take it easy. Calm down." She talked out loud to herself, trying to prepare for their meeting.

When he opened the front door she wondered if her false smile was over the top. But he smiled and seemed happy to see her.

"If I seem a bit distant this evening it's because I'm so tired," she said, giving an advance excuse to cover any obvious changes from her normal mood.

He handed her a glass of chilled white wine and told her it was no problem. They sat together on the long sofa and listened to a Cassandra Wilson CD: cool, laid-back music with a definite nineties soul jazz lick. Karl leant with his back against one of the sofa's arms and pulled her closer to him. He seemed so pleased to see her and so affectionate that she seriously started to wonder if anything Karen had said was true. She wanted to keep her mouth shut about the whole thing, but something inside her needed answers, and now.

They made small talk for a while, but all the time Angela was looking for an opportunity to start probing.

She tutted in a slightly exaggerated way. "Oh, damn! I was supposed to drop off some college books at Karen's this evening and I've just remembered. She'll probably be cursing me ."

"Nah, man. Karen's cool. That's not her style," he reassured.

Angela nodded in agreement and sipped slowly from her glass, waiting to get the timing right. "Oh, I've never asked you how you know Karen. I think I assumed she was an ex-girlfriend." She tried to sound relaxed to the point of indifference, as if she were talking about what was on TV tonight.

"What made you think that?" he asked, his tone giving nothing away.

"Oh, I think it's just the way she talks about you. Women have a sense for these things, you know."

"Well Karen might think she's an ex-girlfriend, but I don't. We had a brief fling a few years ago and that was it. Well, it was more than just that. What I didn't know at the time was that Karen had a long history of mental illness. She became crazy. She threatened to kill herself and even took an overdose one time. But not before she'd phoned me and told me. It was all about getting attention."

He shook his head in disbelief as if the memories were coming back to haunt him. "Another time I was going out with this girl and Karen started phoning up in the middle of the night, warning her to keep away from me. Then one time she went to the police and said I'd raped her. Thank God, the date she gave them was when I was in Germany on business. If that hadn't happened I could have found myself in court. The thing with Karen is that she is a convincing liar, because I think she actually believes some of the nonsense she comes out with. I think that she may have genuinely believed, even though I wasn't with her at the time, that I raped her."

"But, Karl, why do you remain friends with her? She sounds like big trouble. I had no idea she was like that."

"I sometimes ask myself that question. I think it's because I feel guilty. I knew that she was taking our relationship seriously, but for me it was just a bit of fun. When she started to go out of her head, I had to take some responsibility for that. Also, she keeps telling me that she needs me, and I worry that she might really do herself in if I cut all ties."

Angela was starting to feel like she'd been made a fool of. She wanted to get hold of Karen and give her a good, hard slap. How could she have been taken in by this scheming psycho? She wanted to tell Karl the whole story, but was too embarrassed at her own gullibility to recall last night's events. This would be a matter she would take up with Karen in person, and this time round there would be no sympathy.

When she'd arrived at Karl's she had been trying to hide her nervousness about him; now she was doing her utmost to hide the anger she felt towards Karen.

As the evening wore on, Angela was able to put her anger on the back boiler and to try and enjoy her time with Karl. It would, after all, probably be one of the last times they would spend together. The last time they'd met she'd said that she wanted to end things before her husband returned from Europe at the end of the week. It had been an exciting time, she'd told him, but she couldn't take the stress of having an affair while her husband was living in the same house. She had been straight and honest about things, and he'd said he was fine about that. He'd said he was under no illusions about the affair, and saw it simply as a passing moment of pleasure. They'd agreed to enjoy the last few days they had together and then get on with their separate lives.

Karl opened another bottle of wine and filled up Angela's tall, fluted wine glass. The Chardonnay was a particularly good one, but the way Angela was knocking back her glass it was of little importance to her. It was another excuse to unwind with the aid of alcohol. She had recently been drinking more than she usually did, but as she so rarely went out with her husband that also meant very little.

Despite her fatigue, the alcohol was making her feel very randy. She might have to go for weeks or months without proper sex when Malcolm came back, so she thought that she might as well get her fill now.

"Okay, Karl, I've got an idea," she said, sounding rather drunk. "Why don't we play a game where we each ask the other person to help act out our own fantasies? Do you understand what I mean?"

Karl nodded.

"Good. Then explain it to me. Cos I don't know what the fuck I'm talking about." Angela started to laugh loudly at her own silliness, then attempted to compose herself. "Okay, Karl. As I suggested it, I'll let you go first."

He rubbed his chin for a moment, trying to think what he'd like to get his eager volunteer to do first. "Okay. See that empty wine bottle on the table? I want you to use it to play with your pussy, then push it up there."

Angela realised she was more than a little tipsy when she got up from the sofa and promptly fell back down again. Her second attempt was met with greater success, and she quickly stripped of her skirt, shoes and knickers.

Sitting back on the sofa, she teased the lips of her pussy with the slim neck of the bottle, building up lubrication before slowly inserting a few inches of the bottle into her hole. As the lubrication increased it became easier to insert more of the neck into her wetness. She moved it in and out of herself like it was a glass dildo, stopping only to use the fingers of her right hand to hold back her pussy lips so Karl could get a better view of her increasingly swollen clitoris.

Karl was playing it cool, but from the way he wiggled uncomfortably on the sofa it was clear to Angela that his erection was causing him some degree of discomfort in his tight-fitting jeans.

When she had done enough to satisfy the requirements of her dare, she rested the bottle back on the table and contemplated what she wanted from Karl.

Inspiration struck, and she disappeared into the kitchen to explore the possibilities. Shortly she was back with a very satisfied look on her face. "Well, here's one recipe you won't find in Delia Smith's cookbooks." A huge grin spread over her face. "I want you to pour this cream slowly over the head of your penis and let it run over your balls."

Karl laughed with with an incredulous look on his face. "You being serious?" he asked.

With a huge smirk Angela nodded her head vigorously.

Standing up, he started putting on a show for her. Slowly, and in an exaggerated manner, he undid his belt before going to work on the buttons of his jeans. Now he slid his trousers seductively down his legs before stepping out of them. Now he was pulling his white T-shirt up to reveal his well-toned stomach muscles. His smooth, dark-cherry skin contrasted sexily against the white of the shirt and his matching Calvin Kleins.

How Angela loved to see him naked apart from his underwear. It was a great turn-on to see that big, stiff cock of his straining to break free from its 100% cotton prison. In her marketing course her tutors had often stressed the importance of packaging and presentation in the selling of any product, and Karl clearly fulfilled these requirements when it came to himself. He certainly knew how to excite a woman by not showing his penis but by merely working the imagination as to what lay in store.

Angela licked her lips in eager anticipation of the show that awaited her. "Get 'em off," she told him, growing impatient.

He obliged by slipping off his pants and letting his stiff penis spring back with a resounding slap against his abdomen. Pulling back his foreskin to reveal his head in all its throbbing glory, Karl held his penis while his right hand administered to the pouring of the cream. The coldness made his cock jerk, which gave Angela an extra quiver of pleasure as she watched.

An unhurried stream of cream sat on his knob before making its sensual journey down the length of his shaft. Now it continued its journey on to his balls before slipping down his inner thighs.

"Yummy! That sure looks mighty tasty," Angela told him in her best phony Deep-South accent. Thick white cream on firm black cock. It looked like the candy man had climaxed. It was too much of an appetising feast to go to waste, so she took no time in getting down and greedily licking the head of his dick with her warm tongue. Cock never tasted this good, she thought to herself as she licked every drop off the head of his penis, which disappeared into her mouth as she sucked him as if his member were a sweet-tasting ice lolly.

When she had sucked his prick clean she concentrated her sweet tooth on his balls, licking them of the last vestiges of Sainsbury's single cream.

"That was all right, yuh know," Karl concluded, as ever playing it cool. "But my tackle feels like it fell in a honey-pot. I feel sticky as hell. It's my turn now, girlfriend, and I've got just the one. . . I'm going to the bathroom to wipe myself down before some bee comes and stings my dick. But when I get back I wanna see you naked."

"Well, we'll have to see what we can arrange. Will it be worth my while?"

With a twinkle in his eye he walked to the door. "Don't worry, girlfriend. I'm sure it's something you won't forget."

"No bother promise what you cyan deliver, yuh hear?" she jokingly shouted after him.

Such was his eagerness, she had barely removed her top and bra before he was back in the lounge.

"Okay, I hope you're feeling athletic, cos you're gonna need it, girlfriend." He led her by the hand to a clear area of wall space on the other side of the lounge. "How good are you at doing hand-stands?"

It was Angela's turn to sound incredulous. "You're winding me up, right?"

Karl shook his head and pointed to the wall. "You've got that to support you."

"Well, it's been a while, but I was one of the best at gymnastics at school so I'm sure I've still got the knack."

Down on to her hands, and with one deft kick from her feet, Angela was doing a hand-stand with her heels supported against the wall.

"Well, that wasn't too bad. What now?"

Karl turned his head upside down and brought it closer to hers. "If you open your legs slightly wider, I will be with you in one moment. Hol' tight."

It was an interesting perspective of the room, Angela thought as she watched Karl walk back from the kitchen with a bottle of champagne. Wrapping a tea-towel around its neck, he carefully undid the cork which blasted off into a corner of the room.

"I once read a book which had a scene like this in it and I've always said I must try it," he explained.

"Well, whatever you have in mind, yuh bettah hurry cos I cyan stay like dis all night," Angela joked.

The sensation of cold champagne being poured into her pussy gave her quite a shock. The fizzy drink gave a slight stinging feeling. But the perverse nature of it all was such a thrill that this discomfort didn't seem to matter too much.

Karl brought his mouth to her pussy and drank heartily from this most unusual and sensual of vessels. His tongue licked over her clitoris before darting inside.

Whether it was the rush of blood to her head from being upside down or the serious pussy licking she was receiving, Angela didn't know. All she knew was that if she continued being in that position she would pass out. "Enough fantasies," she told him. "I need to be fucked."

From the tone of his slow, heavy breathing, it was clear that Karl was finished for the night. Angela was restless and thirsty. It hadn't been bad sex, it's just that she could have done with more of it, much more of it! Still, it had been fun. The only problem was that it had had the effect of waking her up, not putting her to sleep.

She rolled on to her side in the bed and stared at the flickering flame of the candle in the holder on the bedside table. She hoped this would hypnotise her into sleep, but it also had the reverse effect. It made her feel restless. Maybe a warm drink would help, she thought.

On the way back from the kitchen with a mug of hot chocolate in hand, the light coming from under the door of the spare bedroom which served as Karl's study caught her attention. As she turned the handle, little could she imagine the heartache that lay awaiting her on the other side of that door.

CHAPTER 16

The expression on her friend's face confirmed June's fears. This was something serious.

"My sister has the kids today, so we'll be able to talk. You want a tea or coffee?"

Angela moved the doll on to the floor and made herself comfortable in the armchair by the hi-fi. Despite the lack of small ones, the front room had all the hallmarks of a 'children on board' house. Toys were scattered in happy abandon the length and breadth of the room, and the ripped and scribbled-on copy of the latest Essence told its own story.

June returned from the kitchen with a tray holding two coffee cups. She could see the worried look of anticipation on Angela's face and decided to get straight to the point.

"I didn't want to tell you this on the phone — that's why I thought it best to come over. Listen, Angie, you know that guy you've been seeing? Well, I got some information last night from a friend who used to work for the same firm as him. It turns out that Karl Hendricks didn't leave but was fired for fraud. The bosses didn't want to cause a scandal so they didn't call in the police. He was just told to leave at once.

"Now it turns out that he was found out when a firm of auditors laid a trap for him. Hendricks took the bait and got caught. He claims that there were more senior people involved, and he claims that the auditor knew this but wanted him in particular to take the fall. He claimed it was some conspiracy against him because he was black.

"But what really got him angry was the fact that the auditor was also black. They had some massive argument when he was fired, with Hendricks accusing the guy of being a Judas and a coconut. It got very nasty, and security had to be called. Hendricks was making all kinds of threats to this auditor, who he for some reason saw as being directly responsible for his downfall.

"Well, of course the City is a small place, and word quickly got around. No one was going to employ Hendricks and his City career was over. It turns out that the name of the much-hated auditor was a Mister Malcolm Seymour.

"To me, Angie, all of this is too much of a coincidence, you meeting Karl jus' like so. It don't reason, girl. My money is on the theory that he planned to get back at Malcolm by using you. What better way to get revenge than to mash up the man's marriage? That's how it looks to me."

Angela felt utterly depressed and dejected, but now her discovery of last night at least made sense. "I was around at Karl's last night and I discovered a diary that I'd written everything down in, about my affair with him. He must have taken the diary when he was at my place on Sunday. I never noticed it was missing.

"It was him who suggested I keep a diary for fun. He must have had all this planned from the beginning. He obviously plans to tell all to Malcolm, and the diary was going to be part of the 'evidence'."

As Angela thought things out it was obvious that what Karen had told her was the truth. The sheer cunning and ruthlessness of Karl made her shiver. She wondered what he was capable of and what limits he would go to to get his revenge. She desperately didn't want him to have the satisfaction of wrecking her marriage — because, knowing how Malcolm would react to news of her infidelity, wreck is exactly what would happen.

"June, what the hell am I going to do?"

CHAPTER 17

It was one of the most unpleasant experiences she had ever gone through. It made her feel resentment to her very core, to the point where she felt at one point almost physically ill. She now really knew how a prostitute must feel. She had lain there and pretended that the thrusting and groaning was exciting her. While in her mind all she could do was hope it would be over quickly. Fortunately her prayers were answered and he was soon shooting his load. Now all she would have to wait for was for him to fall into a deep sleep.

She had explained her disappearance the night before with the excuse that she missed her home. He didn't say anything, and if he had noticed the fact that her diary was no longer in his possession he certainly wasn't letting on.

As his breathing got heavier, Angela prepared herself for the task at hand. Malcolm was due back tomorrow afternoon so she only had one shot to get this right. June had been amazing, and now it was time to see if she could pull it off.

The receiver was shaking in her hand as she pushed the last digit of his phone number. She looked at her watch. Malcolm was due home in the next hour.

"Hi, Karl speaking."

"Listen, Karl. I haven't got much time, so I'll be brief. After this call I want you to go and lift the top off your toilet cistern. Inside you will find, taped to the top, a small packet containing cocaine. Now, somewhere else in the house is a large quantity of coke, about three thousand pounds' worth. It is extremely well hidden and to be honest you have little chance of finding it.

"If you make any attempt to contact me again, or to inform my husband or anyone else of our affair, I will contact the police and let them know of your cocaine dealing and, of course, where you hide your supply. I will also be able to supply the names of three people who will swear under oath that you have supplied them with cocaine.

"If any of the threatening letters or phone calls occur, I will be forced to do the same.

"Goodbye, Karl."

Those were the last words Angela Seymour ever spoke to Karl Hendricks. During the next three months she held her breath, not daring to hope that she had pulled it off. But as time went by she realised that Karl was not stupid enough to try anything.

Of course there was no other cocaine planted in the house, but after finding the first packet, could Karl have really taken the chance? June had arranged for a friend to sort out a connection with some rude bwoy he knew, and Angela had driven up to Harlesden to purchase the coke that day.

And what of Malcolm? Well, maybe he sensed that something had gone down in his absence, because he suddenly started paying Angela a whole lot more attention, and their relationship got a great deal better.

Angela threw away the diary, graduated from university, remembered the sex, and concluded that, once in a lifetime, every woman really does deserve an adventure.

Books with ATTITUDE

THE RAGGA & THE ROYAL by Monica Grant Streetwise Leroy Massop and The Princess of Wales get it together in this light-hearted romp. £5.99

JAMAICA INC. by Tony Sewell Jamaican Prime Minister, David Cooper, is shot down as he addresses the crowd at a reggae 'peace' concert. Who pulled the trigger and why? £5.99

LICK SHOT by Peter Kalu A black detective in an all white police force! £5.99

PROFESSOR X by Peter Kalu When a black American radical visits the UK to expose a major corruption scandal, only a black cop can save him from the assasin's bullet. £5.99

SINGLE BLACK FEMALE by Yvette Richards Three career women end up sharing a house together and discover they all share the same problem-MEN! £5.99

MOSS SIDE MASSIVE by Karline Smith Manchester drugs gangs battle it out. £5.99

OPP by Naomi King How deep does friendship go when you fancy your best friend's man? Find out in this hot bestseller! £5.99

COP KILLER by Donald Gorgon When his mother is shot dead by the police, Lloyd Baker goes for revenge. Controversial but compulsive reading. £4.99

BABY FATHER/ BABY FATHER 2 by Patrick Augustus Four men come to terms with parenthood in this smash hit and its sequel. £5.99

WHEN A MAN LOVES A WOMAN by Patrick Augustus The greatest romance story ever...probably. £5.99

WICKED IN BED by Sheri Campbell Michael Hughes believes in 'loving and leaving 'em' when it comes to women. But if you play with fire you're gonna get burnt! £5.99

FETISH by Victor Headley The acclaimed author of 'Yardie', 'Excess', and 'Yush!' serves another gripping thriller where appearances can be very deceiving! £5.99

UPTOWN HEADS by R.K. Byers Hanging with the homeboys and homegirls in uptown New York. A superb, vibrant novel about the black American male. £5.99

GAMES MEN PLAY by Michael Maynard What do the men get up to when their women aren't around? A novel about black men behaving outrageously! £5.99

DANCEHALL by Anton Marks. Reggae deejay Simba Ranking meets an uptown woman. He thinks everything is level vibes, until her husband finds out. £5.99

BABY MOTHER by Andrea Taylor. Life really is full of little surprises! £6.99

OBEAH by Colin Moone Mysterious murders and family feuds in rural Jamaica, where truth is stranger than fiction. *Winner of Xpress Yourself '95 writing competition!* £5.99

AVAILABLE FROM WH SMITH AND ALL GOOD BOOKSHOPS

CARIBBEAN CATERERS & TAKE AWAY

"The Taste Without The Expense!" (TM)

**Wedding Parties & Luncheons
all catered for - get an instant quote**

CALL THE HOTLINE NOW!
0831 423 163

265e New Cross Rd
New Cross
SE14
(next to New Cross
Gate train station)
0181 694 1745

9 George Lane
Catford
SE13
(opposite
George pub)
0181 690 9167

293 Sydenham Road
Sydenham
SE26
(opposite Library &
Home Park)
0181 776 5868

23 Lewisham Road
Greenwich SE13
(corner of
Blackheath Hill)
0181 691 4149

7b Dartmouth Road
Forest Hill SE23
(near B.R. station)
incorporating sandwich bar
0181 699 6144

DELIVERY SERVICE AVAILABLE

OPENING TIMES
Monday - Saturday 10 am - Midnight
Sunday 1.30 - 10.00pm
(Confirm details locally may alter)

"Once the accepted standard has been acheived
its time to set another - **CUMMIN' UP**"

BARBER'S

		ADULT	OAP/CHILD
DEF ROW CUT	short back and sides	£6.00	£5.00
BUCK WILD CUT	design/pattern	£10.00	£7.00
LO KEY CUT	one level one	£5.00	£4.00
ONE X CUT	bald	£5.00	£4.00
PAROLE CUT	afro	£6.00	£5.00
HANDS UP CUT	flat-top	£7.00	£5.00
REPRIEVE CUT	hair, beard & moustache	£12.00	£7.00
ELEGAL CUT	wash and cut	£12.00	£7.00

0181 289 3787   **0181 289 3785**

133-135 Maple Road, Penge SE20

HAMMOCK LEISURE HOLIDAYS

We can arrange your accomodation throughout theCaribbean

We can arrange:
- Hotels
- Villas

- Honeymoon Accomodation
- Group Accomodation
- Cricket, Carnivals and events

SPECIALISTS TO THE CARIBBEAN

Tel no: 0171 423 9400
Freecall: 0800 018 4700

Wickham House, 10 Cleveland Way
London E1 4TR

Now at last a complete range of hair care and treatment products that use 100% natural ingredients formulated to leave your hair looking healthier and more beautiful than ever before.

Products available in three treatment ranges:-

* **RELAXING**
* **CLEANSE AND CONDITION**
* **SHINE**

Available in stores throughout the UK including selected branches of Superdrug, Sainsbury's and Tesco.